Soul Awakening

Book I of the Dacque Chronicles

by
DOUG SIMPSON

Copyright © 2012 Doug Simpson

Soul Awakening was first published in the United States in 2011 By BookLocker.com

This book is a work of fiction. Names, characters, businesses, organizations, places, events and incidents either are the product of the author's imagination or are used fictitiously. Any resemblance to actual persons, living or deceased, or actual events is entirely coincidental.

5 PRINCE PUBLISHING AND BOOKS, LLC
PO Box 16507
Denver, CO 80216
www.5PrinceBooks.com

ISBN 13: 978-1939217-07-3 ISBN 10: 1939217075
Soul Awakening
Doug Simpson
Copyright Doug Simpson 2012
Published by 5 Prince Publishing

Front Cover art by Viola Estrella
All rights reserved. No part of this book may be used or reproduced in any manner whatsoever without written permission, except in the case of brief quotations, reviews, and articles. For any other permission please contact 5 Prince Publishing and Books, LLC.

First Printing by 5 Prince Publishing November 2012

5 PRINCE PUBLISHING AND BOOKS, LLC.

DEDICATION

Soul Awakening is dedicated to the late Edgar Cayce, the individual primarily responsible for my own soul awakening.

ACKNOWLEDGMENTS

First and foremost, I would like to thank the wonderful people at the Edgar Cayce Foundation, and Edgar Cayce's Association for Research and Enlightenment, both located in Virginia Beach, Virginia, for their never-ending advice, support, proofreading and encouragement.

I would also like to thank my Editor Connie Kline and all of the other wonderful, hardworking staff members at 5 Prince Publishing for their support, assistance, advice, and faith in me and the Soul Awakening manuscript.

Lastly, I would like to express heart-felt thanks to my wife, Marion, for her assistance, advice, encouragement, and definitely her patience, as I devoted the hundreds of hours required to write and perfect the manuscript that became Soul Awakening.

Doug Simpson

Chapter 1
Morning Routine

Dacque shuffled along the dimly-lit hallway in his aging leather slippers and summer pajamas, only partially concealed by his untied new housecoat, a gift from his only granddaughter. He headed off towards the kitchen to his standard dose of pills and health food mulligan. With step one in his breakfast routine dispensed with, he made his way to the door of his apartment, held his housecoat around him with one hand, and with the other, quickly opened the door and snatched his morning newspaper from the scuffed, hardwood floor of the third floor corridor.

Newspaper read, breakfast completed, coffee cup empty, and now dressed, Dacque strode towards the elevator and his morning walk, curious, as always, to discover what welcome new adventures this beautiful spring morning might bring into his life. Routine was fine for the insignificant, mundane first-hour or so of each day, but the unknown adventures that he eagerly looked forward to on his daily walk around the small city of Anywhere, was his primary impetus to climb out of bed every morning.

Chapter 2
The Woman In The Park

Dacque exited the 7th Street Apartment Complex and turned north on 7th Street. The previous day he had walked south, and as he had no specific errands to attend to, then today's adventure must be awaiting him somewhere to the north. As he approached Olive Avenue the street light turned red, indicating, based on previous experience, that he was supposed to cross 7th Street, so Dacque obediently continued west on Olive, unencumbered for three blocks, until once again directed by another red light at 10th Street. Crossing Olive Avenue and proceeding north on 10th, Dacque began to suspect where he was being led by the Powers-That-Be, but that was fine with him. He cherished his walks through MacDunnah Park, and the opportunity they provided for him to listen to the melodious songbirds that either resided in or frequented the lush gardens of this oasis in the middle of chaos. Dacque dodged the sparse traffic at Lime Avenue, crossed to the west side of 10th Street, and entered the Park.

The colorful flowers as well as the flowering bushes, whose names he never seemed to be able to remember for long, were coming into full bloom and the aroma was heaven sent. There were a few folks around, but because it was a school day the terrain was reasonably peaceful. Dacque took the East Path, parallel to 10th Street, and strolled along in seventh-heaven. At the Central, East-West Path, he veered left towards the center of the park where the most-beautiful flowers and abundance of shaded benches resided.

Opting for the Circular Path, Dacque noticed a woman on a bench to his right, with her face in her hands. As he shortened the distance between them, he could hear her sobbing, but decided that it was most-appropriate that he discreetly walk on by, pretending to ignore her. Fat chance! In his head, as clearly as if it were spoken in his ear by some invisible elf perched on his shoulder, he heard, "Oh no you don't! Get back there!"

Dacque commenced an immediate U-turn, without signaling, and was fortunate that he had no tail-gaiting foot-traffic to wreak havoc for. Backtracking to the woman on the bench, he stood in front of her for a long moment. When it became obvious that she was unaware of his presence, Dacque slowly approached the bench and settled in beside her. "Are you okay, Miss?"

The woman lifted her face from her hands, obviously startled, and Dacque immediately noticed the blood-shot eyes and tears trickling down her cheeks. "I'm just wonderful!" she blurted out sarcastically, "Please leave me alone."

"I can't do that! God told me to help you!"

The young woman glared at Dacque, open-mouthed. "What did you just say?"

"God ...... told ...... me ...... to ...... help ...... you!"

The two of them silently sat there, sharing a park bench on a quiet spring morning, and stared into each other's eyes.

Finally, the young woman wiped the tears from her cheeks and said softly, "Say that one more time so that I'm perfectly clear as to what I think I am hearing."

"God told me to help you. He occasionally leads me to people who need His help."

The staring session resumed. Eventually, Dacque could detect the faintest smile beginning to appear at the edges of the young woman's makeup-less lips. "I am certainly not prepared to believe anything that you are telling me, and fortunately for you, you do not appear to be a dangerous character, so I will give you an opportunity to convince me that you are not an escapee from the loony-bin."

"Fair enough! I accept the challenge!" Dacque replied. "As I walked by, I noticed you with your face in your hands, and then heard your sobs, but I kept on walking. Then, I heard, as clear as I hear you now, 'Oh no you don't! Get back there!'"

"And that's how God speaks to you?"

"At times, especially if I am ignoring His previous instructions. I knew, from previous experience, that I was directed here today for a specific purpose, and when I saw you in distress I suspected that you were the reason I was led here, yet I chose to walk on by. Now and then, God also pays me visits when I am asleep or in a semiconscious state. I can't swear to you that it is God. It is still difficult for me to believe that God would actually bother to deal with me directly. It could be an Angel or one of God's other helpers. The instructions I receive always involve performing good deeds, never anything evil."

"Okay, I'm still not prepared to admit that I believe you, but I will listen to you, at least for a few minutes. So, how are you supposed to help me?"

"I don't actually know, yet, because I do not know why you were crying. I also have not received any instructions as to what I am to do."

"I'm really not in the habit of sharing my problems with total strangers on park benches."

"I should hope not. I am not asking you to tell me anything about yourself, just why you were crying? Do you have a pain in your belly? Did a pigeon poop on your head? What caused the tears to flow on this beautiful spring morning?"

The young woman smiled. Dacque thought it was a beautiful smile. "Nothing like that. I guess you could say that I am just down, depressed. It was such a beautiful morning. I wanted to get out of my apartment and enjoy some of this wonderful spring weather, but after I sat here for a short while my problems seemed to return and my bony shoulders were too weak to support them."

"Are your legs okay?" Dacque inquired.

"Yes, just fine. Why?"

"I love to walk around this beautiful park. I come here often. Instead of sitting here and talking, what do you say we walk and talk?"

"That's fine with me."

Dacque stood up and raised his left elbow away from his side. The young woman understood the gesture and looped her arm around his. "Anyone watching us will just assume that you are taking your old Grandpa for a morning stroll." The woman gently squeezed his arm in reply. "Okay, tell me about this big weight you are carrying on your shoulders," he said, as they sauntered along the paved pathway.

"I am a legal secretary, a recently unemployed legal secretary. I moved here to Anywhere about six months ago, from Dallas, when my boyfriend was transferred here, and quickly found a job in a local legal office. Then, a couple of months ago, my boyfriend informed me that he was moving back to New York, where his ex-wife and two little kids live, with the intention of attempting a reconciliation. Obviously, I was not part of his new plan.

"I decided to keep the small apartment that we shared, as I had a good job here, I really like living in Anywhere, and to just wait and see how things progressed. They got worse. About a month later, the lawyer whose secretary I was, was transferred to another office in Miami, and, as the most recent hire, I became surplus. They did give me a nice three-month severance package, much more than they had to, but I was now unemployed.

"For the past month I have been trying diligently to obtain other reasonable employment, but with no luck. I am obviously not destitute, yet anyway, but deserted here in Anywhere with no relatives or close friends. This morning, on this beautiful day, I just could not hold-in all of the pressure any longer, and the tear-dam burst wide open."

"I understand," Dacque said, sympathetically.

"Has God got any Miracles up His sleeve for me?" the woman asked after an elongated pause.

Dacque laughed. "Not that He has informed me of, yet, but I have no doubts whatsoever that He is working on it this very second. Do you know how to pray?"

"I guess so, but I must admit that I have not had much practice at it in a long while."

"That's not a significant problem. When you settle into bed tonight, say a little prayer. Explain your current problems to God, and ask Him to work out a solution for you. Do not say just one prayer, but keep praying over and over again until you fall off to sleep. Can you do that?"

"I guess so."

"Good."

Dacque and the young woman walked around the park, arm in arm, for almost two hours, chatting casually and getting cautiously acquainted. With noon approaching, Dacque asked if he could treat her to lunch, and she accepted. After a very enjoyable lunch, they said their goodbyes outside of the restaurant. Dacque handed her a card, his card with his name, address and telephone number on it, that he had printed-up years before when God first started talking, or sending messages, to him, or maybe that was when he first started listening to what God was saying. The young woman, who appeared to Dacque to be in her late twenties, never told him her name, address, or telephone number, which was fine with him. A young lady, alone in the city, had to be careful about these things. If she wanted to meet him again, he had opened the door for her, and that was all he could do.

Chapter 3
Dani

The next day, Dacque followed his habitual, morning routine pretty much to the letter, and turned south onto 7th Street a few minutes after nine o'clock. Two steps into his southern trek he was greeted by the now-familiar voice, "You are going the wrong way!" Dacque was not-the-least-bit surprised by this communication, and commenced an abrupt about-face. As he approached Olive Avenue, the street light turned red, just like the day before, propelling him across 7th Street on the green and continuing west. He was pretty sure he knew exactly where he was being led, so another red light at 10th came as no big shock.

Dacque entered MacDunnah Park and retraced his steps from the day before. As he entered the central circle, he could see the young legal secretary sitting on the same bench as yesterday, watching his approach.

"Good morning, Dacque. I was uncertain whether you would walk this way this morning?" she said.

"To be perfectly truthful, I headed south at first, but I was abruptly advised that I was going the wrong way."

"You certainly have Powerful Connections."

"You don't know the half of it, trust me," Dacque responded, accompanied by a smile. "Shall we walk again?"

The young woman stood up, and once more took Dacque's arm, giving it an affectionate squeeze, and they were off for a morning stroll.

"You appear to be in a much better mood this morning?" Dacque commented.

"Much, much, much better, thanks to you, and your Connections, which truthfully I still have great difficulty trying to rationalize through my humanized brain."

Dacque laughed. "Trust me, I understand. I was there once myself, and not really that many years ago, but that's a story that will have to wait for another time and place."

They walked along in silence for a few minutes, enjoying the pleasures that Mother Nature had blessed them with on this perfect spring morning. "I followed your advice last night when I got into bed, and prayed and prayed until I fell asleep."

"How did you sleep?"

"Like a baby. Best sleep I've had in years. You would not believe, actually you probably would, how happy and relaxed I was when I awoke this morning. I pinched myself to see if I was dreaming."

"That's fabulous! You are off to a great start. I do not want to sound redundant, but you really should follow the same approach every night."

"I will. I may not understand what is going on, but I have already understood the benefits. When I return home, later, I intend to eagerly pursue my future employment opportunities. My attitude has almost-instantly flip-flopped from very negative and frustrated to positive, positive, and more positive.

There is a job out there waiting for me, somewhere. I just have to find it."

The excitement in her voice and attitude was unmistakable. Dacque was thrilled. "You have caught on to this really quickly. I am impressed!"

"I'm no dummy! I was down, with two quick and unexpected strikes against me in a row, but I wasn't out, by any means. I'm not going to settle for just a base hit, I'm searching for a home run."

Dacque smiled, and was pleased that his new, now-friendly acquaintance had some understanding of baseball lingo.

They walked along in silence for a while, and the young woman reached into the pocket of her blouse. She held up a piece of paper. "My name is Dani. This is my phone number. It is a cell phone number. Just in case you want to get in touch one day."

Dacque glanced at the paper and noticed the spelling of her name. No Surname, just Dani. "Thank you, Dani." He slid the paper into his shirt pocket, and told himself, silently, to move it to his wallet, later.

Dani and Dacque spent the rest of the morning casually strolling around the beautiful park, watching the birds and the squirrels and enjoying the sweet fragrances emanating from Mother Nature's Miracles. There was so much more that he needed to explain to Dani, but he knew, from experience, that he had to educate her, patiently, one step at a time, in life on the other side, the world that most humans could not see or hear and habitually found it inconceivable to believe even existed.

Dacque treated her to lunch once more. He enjoyed her refreshing company so much that he hated to see her leave, but he was fully aware that she had a long life ahead of her that she needed, at this point, to resurrect from the ashes of the previous two months. He knew he would see her again, probably soon, but he had to back away for the present.

Outside of the restaurant, Dani stepped close to Dacque, kissed him on the cheek, and gave him a long, strong, embrace. "Thank you for popping into my life. I hate to think of where I might have tumbled to if you had not come along, or should that be, was sent along? I will start thanking God in my prayers for sending you to me. I will not try to meet you again for a while, and instead devote my full attention to finding another job. We have each other's number, when needed. Bye for now."

Chapter 4
The Tumble

Dacque turned south for his morning walk, curiously wondering if his destination would be redirected once again. Not this time. He encountered his first red light at Lemon Avenue, and did not wait, venturing east along Lemon. His next red light appeared well into the downtown core, at 2nd Street, but conveniently changed to green as he approached the corner. Dacque did not miss a stride and proceeded to cross 2nd Street, until his attention was directed to his right by a blaring car horn.

The next thing that Dacque could recall was someone helping him back to his feet and the merciless throbbing in his right knee.

"Are you alright, sir?" a tall, football-player-built man in an obviously expensive suit asked. He had assisted Dacque back up onto his left foot. Standing on his right foot was not an option, at least for the moment, anyway.

"I think so, but my right knee is killing me."

"My office building is right here on the corner. Let me help you in there. There are a number of chairs and couches in the foyer. You can rest up a while until you are feeling better," the well-dressed man suggested.

The Good-Samaritan assisted Dacque to hobble into the foyer of the office building, and eased him onto a couch.

"Thank you, very much," Dacque said. "I can move my knee a bit now, so hopefully nothing is broken."

"That's good news. I see you scraped your left palm. Let's check and see if you have any more scrapes or bruises?" Dacque held out his forearms and both of them carried out an inspection, spotting, at approximately the same instant, a companion scrape on his right elbow. "Neither one of those looks too life-threatening," he told Dacque. "We had better have a look at that right knee." Dacque pulled up the leg of his slacks. There was another scrape on the knee, but more disturbing was the swelling that was already blossoming around the kneecap. "I don't like that swelling," the young man stated, "can I call you an ambulance or a taxi? You should have that knee looked at."

"I'll be fine," Dacque assured him. "I'll just sit here a while until I feel better and then be on my way."

"I wish I could spend more time with you, but I need to get upstairs for an important meeting that starts in a few minutes. Are you certain that there is nothing more I can do for you?"

"I'll be fine. Thank you for all of your help." Dacque watched the well-dressed gentleman head for the elevator and disappear through the open door in a crowd of people. He sat there for a while on the couch, and watched the workers hurry-by on their way to the elevators, while cautiously flexing his sore knee to test its mobility.

Some minutes later, a well-dressed, middle-aged woman hurried out of one of the elevators with a strange looking box under her arm, and walked towards Dacque. She sat down beside him.

"My name is Sara. My boss, Mr. Winston, asked me to come down and see if you were still here, and if you were, to clean-up your scrapes." She opened up the first-aid kit.

"They're not serious. I'll be fine."

"Never mind!" Sara said with authority. "You sound just like my father. Let's see those scrapes."

Sara doctored the scrapes on his palm and elbow. "Alright, let's have a look at the knee, next." Dacque pulled up the leg on his slacks again, and Sara also disinfected that scrape. "There is a lot of swelling there. Mr. Winston said you would not go to the hospital, but you better have someone look at it. Is there anyone we can call to come and get you?"

Dacque started to shake his head, but stopped. He reached for his wallet and handed Sara the piece of paper with Dani's name and cell phone number on it. "She may be home and could come and get me."

Sara stood up. "I will call her. What is your name, sir?"

"Dacque, spelled D .. a .. c .. q .. u .. e."

When Sara exited the elevator on the eighth floor, she was surprised to see Max Winston in the outer-office. "What happened to your meeting?"

"The boys have some points to settle amongst themselves, so I suggested that they call me when they have reached an agreement. How is Mr. Wounded-Knee?"

"I doctored his scrapes, but the knee needs to be looked at. He gave me the name of someone to call, but did not say who she was. I'll call her."

"Why don't you let me call her? I can give her the details on how he fell. Did he mention his name?"

Sara handed Max the paper. "Dacque, spelled D .. a .. c .. q .. u.. e."

Max took the paper and went into his office.

"Hello!" a cheerful voice said at the other end of the line.

"Hello, is this Dani?"

"Yes."

"You don't know me, Dani. My name is Max Winston. Are you related to an elderly gentleman named Dacque?"

"We are not related, but I know him. Is there something wrong?"

"He had a little accident this morning, downtown. Nothing serious, but he banged up his right knee pretty good."

"Was he hit by a car?"

"No. He was crossing 2nd Street at Lemon. I was a couple of steps behind him, and some guy leaned on his car horn out in the intersection. I suspect Dacque was distracted just as he was stepping up onto the far curb and probably stubbed his toe, throwing himself onto the sidewalk, face first."

"Oh my Lord!"

"My secretary doctored his scrapes, but his knee is rather swollen. He refused to go to the hospital, but he gave her a paper with your name and number on it. If you are able to, I would like to suggest that you pick him up and take him to the hospital for a check-up, whether he likes it or not."

"I'm on my way. Thank you, Max, for all of your assistance."

Max gave Dani the directions to his office building. He suggested that she approach it from the east and stop directly in front of the double doors in the no-parking zone, which many drivers used to pick-up or drop-off passengers.

Chapter 5
The Hospital

Dani stopped her car in the no-parking zone in front of the Mackie Building, the building where Max Winston worked. She opted not to leave the car running with the keys in it, but instead, opened up the front passenger door to indicate, to any of the Anywhere Parking Authority officers who might chance by, that someone would shortly be entering the open door.

Dacque was happy to see Dani zip through the double doors.

"Are you okay, Dacque?" she inquired, with obvious concern.

"Pretty much, I think. My right knee is rather sore, but the rest of me, is fine."

"My car is waiting right outside the double doors," Dani advised him. "Let me help you walk out there." She heard a door open behind her, and spotted a woman entering the building. "Excuse me, Miss, but could I impose on you for a moment or two, to hold that door open, while I assist my injured friend here to walk to my waiting car, out front?"

"Certainly," the woman responded, and retreated to the door.

Dani thanked the woman as they exited the building and she quickly had Dacque stashed away in the front seat of her vehicle. She turned the car right, onto 2nd Street, and right again on Orange Avenue.

"This isn't the way to my place," Dacque advised her.

"I know. Max Winston told me you refused his advice to go to the hospital, but in case it has not yet occurred to you, you are my hostage, and you are going to the hospital to have that knee checked."

Dacque frowned, noticeably, but held his tongue.

Dani turned right again on Main Street, and drove a number of blocks before reaching the entrance to Anywhere District Hospital. She stopped at the Emergency Room door. The security guard was on his feet immediately, but before he could get one word out of his mouth, Dani hollered over the roof of her car, "Could you please fetch a wheelchair? He may have a broken kneecap."

The security guard hurried back inside and Dani went to assist Dacque to get out of the front seat. The returning guard helped settle him into the wheelchair.

"If you could wheel him inside for me, I will move my car to the parking lot."

"Good idea," he replied, and wheeled Dacque away.

It took over an hour before the emergency-room staff was able to get to Dacque, and after he was processed through the system, a nurse wheeled him off to one of the individual waiting rooms. "I will come and get you when you are able to join him," she said to Dani.

Dani spent at least another hour in the waiting room flipping through magazines she really had no interest in reading, until she finally heard a woman call, "Is there a Dani out here?" As Dani stood up, she was advised that she could join Dacque in waiting room Number 2.

Dacque looked up as Dani entered the room, and his somber facial expression morphed into a slight grin.

"How's it going?" Dani asked.

"A Doctor looked at my knee for a minute, and said that they had better take some pictures to be sure, but he does not think anything is broken. I'm just waiting for them to wheel me off to the x-ray room."

"Well, that's pretty good news for starters," Dani responded, not really knowing what else she could say to cheer him up.

"It's almost two o'clock. Did you get anything to eat?" Dacque inquired.

"No, I'm not really hungry. Did you?"

"No, neither am I."

Dani heard her cell phone chime, inside her purse. "I have no idea who that is, but I better check it in case somebody is replying to one of my employment applications."

"By all means," Dacque replied.

"Hello."

"Hello, is this Dani?"

"Yes."

"This is Max Winston, again. I had a few free minutes, and I wanted to check up on how you made out with Dacque, today?"

"Hello, Max. We are in a waiting room at Anywhere District Hospital, next to the main waiting room. A Doctor looked at the knee cap and does not think it is broken, but they are going to x-ray it shortly, just to make sure."

"The news could be much worse, I guess. If you don't mind, I'll check back later for an update?"

"Anytime, Max. Thank you for all of your help, today, and your concerns. Bye for now."

An orderly wheeled Dacque out of the room for his x-ray, and returned him to a waiting Dani, some twenty minutes later.

"Well?" she asked.

"They didn't tell me anything," he advised her.

A Doctor or intern eventually joined them. "We are going to move you to a semi-private room, shortly, and you will probably spend the night with us. Someone will give you a shot to try and bring the swelling down a bit, and a knee specialist will drop in this evening to have a look at your knee, after the swelling has some time to go down."

Chapter 6
Good News

The orderly removed Dacque's half-finished dinner tray. Dani had encouraged him to eat more, but he could not make himself do it. They both watched the second hand on the clock tick one slow tick at a time, as the hour hand approached eight. Dani's cell phone chimed. "Hello."

"Hello Dani. It's Max again. How did Dacque make out today?"

"They have moved him into Room 222, and a knee specialist is supposed to check him over fairly soon, apparently. They told Dacque that he may be kept here overnight, but we gather that depends on the word of the specialist."

"I am just finishing up some paperwork at the office, and if Dacque feels up to it, I would like to pop in for a few minutes on my way home."

"I'm sure he would love to see you again, Max," she said, her eyes on Dacque's vertically-motioning head, as he attentively monitored their conversation. "He just nodded in the affirmative."

"Super. I should be there within fifteen minutes." He hung up.

"He said within fifteen minutes," Dani advised Dacque. "Max sounds like a very nice gentleman. What does he do?"

"I have absolutely no idea, but he, as well as Sara his secretary, certainly paid more attention to me this morning than your average Joe or Josie would have. I immediately liked him."

True to his word, Max walked through the door, to Room 222, within fifteen minutes. "Hi, I'm Max, and I presume you are Dani?" he said, and warmly shook her hand, before turning his attention to the wounded-warrior. "Hello, again Dacque. Is there any good news, yet?"

Dacque and Dani started to fill Max in on more of the details of their long, trying day, but were suddenly interrupted by a nurse and Doctor entering the room behind them.

"Good evening everyone. I am Doctor Schwartz, and I would like to take a few minutes and examine Mr. LaRose's ailing knee, in private."

Dani and Max walked out into the corridor. "Have you tried the cafeteria food, here?" Max asked Dani. "I have not had any dinner yet, and I just realized how hungry I am getting."

"No, I wasn't in the mood to eat earlier, so I have no idea how good or bad it is."

"What do you say we go see if we can locate the cafeteria? I'll buy you dinner," Max said.

"I should be buying you dinner, for all of the kindness you bestowed upon Dacque, today."

"Sorry. I asked you first. You have to be quick to get ahead of me."

"I'll remember that," Dani assured Max as they walked along.

Max and Dani located the cafeteria in the basement of the hospital. There was a handful of hospital staff, as well as visitors, scattered throughout the seating area, but the serving staff was gone for the day. The hungry duo walked over to examine the choices offered in the vending machines, and both ultimately settled for egg-salad sandwiches, slices of cherry pie, and cans of ice tea.

They selected a table in one corner of the cafeteria, and immediately proceeded to devour their sandwiches. "Dacque and I both know where your office building is located, but we realized earlier that neither of us knew what your occupation was?" Dani said, starting the conversation.

"I'm a lawyer, a corporate lawyer in mergers and acquisitions. What about you?"

"I'm actually a legal secretary, currently unemployed, after the lawyer I worked for was transferred to Miami and I was declared surplus. Know of any openings in your office?" Dani asked jokingly.

"None that I am aware of," Max replied, "but I promise that I will keep my ears open."

"Thank you. I'd certainly appreciate that," Dani assured him, and commenced to dig into her slice of cherry pie.

"You told me, when I called you this morning, that you were not a relative of Dacque's. I'm just curious, and I really don't need to know, but where do you fit into the picture?" Max asked.

Dani was caught off-guard by the question. She certainly was not willing to tell him the entire story, but she was also not prepared to lie to him, either. "I guess the proper term for our association is walking partners. Dacque faithfully walks around various sections of the city, every morning after breakfast and usually until lunch-time. One day, after I had been laid-off, we met by accident in MacDunnah Park, started chatting for a few minutes, and then spent a couple of hours walking and talking together. He is really an interesting character, with emphasis on both the interesting and the character, as you may have already deduced. We have walked together one other day at the Park, not pre-arranged, and we then exchanged phone numbers. I suspect that it was my piece of paper that Dacque passed on to your secretary this morning?"

"That's likely a good assumption." Max added.

Dani drained the last drop of moisture from her ice-tea can. "Thank you for dinner. I should get back upstairs and see if I can take Dacque home tonight, or not."

"I'll come with you."

Room 222 had only one occupant when Max and Dani arrived. Dacque, still in the hospital bed, certainly did not look elated but neither did he appear depressed.

"Okay, road-runner," Dani teased him, "what kind of shape are you in?"

"The Doc thinks it is only a bruise and fluid buildup. He will check on me again tomorrow morning, and if nothing has gotten worse, I will get booted out the door."

"Wonderful," Dani declared. "Call me and I will come and get you."

"You'd better, young lady, seeing as it was you who took me hostage and deposited me here," Dacque teased back.

"I should be on my way home, now," Max interceded. "I will call you sometime tomorrow, when I get a chance, Dani, for an update," and edged towards the door. "Have a good night, Dacque."

"Thank you again, for dinner," Dani said. "Talk to you tomorrow."

Dani turned her attention back to Dacque. "Is there anything else I can do or get for you, my friend, before I head off to home myself?"

"I need another paper with your phone number on it. I seem to have misplaced the other one."

Dani smiled as she reached for the pad in her purse. She could not be certain whether Dacque was teasing her, or whether he actually did not remember that he had given the original paper to Sara. It did not matter.

Chapter 7
A New Emergency

Dani finished-up in the shower and slipped into her nightgown. She decided to give her hair a few minutes to air-dry, before taking the blower to it. As she reached for the television remote, her cell phone chimed. Immediately, she assumed there was a new problem with Dacque.

"Hello."

"Hello, Dani. It's Max, one more time. I am so sorry to be calling you this late, but I have my own emergency. I just got off of the phone with Sara, my secretary, the one who doctored Dacque's scrapes this morning. She just received a call that her father suffered a major heart attack this evening, and she will be on the first flight that she can locate for Chicago. Our firm has a temporary-help service that they often call for replacements. Some of their temps are good, and some of them are rather short on experience. Would you have any interest in filling in for Sara until she returns? She indicated that she might stay in Chicago for a few weeks, if required. She has vacation time banked so she does not need to rush back."

"I would love to!" Dani declared. "I think you were still there, but I did tell Dacque that I would pick him up tomorrow, when he received the all-clear."

"That's not a problem. I can do without a secretary for an hour or two, but not a few weeks. You can leave whenever he calls."

"Okay, I'm on-board!"

"Great. Thank you for coming to my rescue. Could you be at the office - the firm has the entire eighth floor of the Mackie Building - around eight-thirty? That will give me time to get you oriented, and then I can take you over to Payroll at nine, to fill out their paperwork. Will that work for you?"

"That will work fine. What do I do for parking down there?"

"Most of us just park in the Anywhere Parking Garage at the corner 3rd and Lemon, and walk to the office. We get a break if we pay by the month, but they charge ten dollars a day. Why don't you just pay the ten dollars, and I will tell Payroll to pay you an extra ten dollars for each day you work. I will also tell them to pay you at Sara's rate of pay, but I do not know exactly what that is."

"You don't have to pay my parking."

"Let's just think of it as a bonus for bailing me out of a jam on no notice at all. I said it first. Remember? You have to be fast to beat me to the punch."

"I'm learning very quickly. Okay, parking is on the firm. Is there anything else I should know, tonight?"

"Not that I can think of," Max replied. "Have a good sleep."

"I will," Dani lied. "Goodnight Max and thank you." When Dani signed off, she wanted to jump up and down and scream for joy, but at that time of night it was not advisable. She settled for, "Thank you, Lord, for taking such good care of me."

Chapter 8
Dani's Surprise

Dani was keyboarding away like a champion, when she heard her cell phone chime. She looked up at the clock. Ten minutes after eleven. Must be Dacque, looking for his ride, she surmised. Her first day at Brown, Kluzewski, McIntosh and Partners, had gone so smooth that she felt like she could never have been on the unemployment line for almost two months.

"Hello."

"Good morning Dani. They sprung me. Can you come and get me, please?"

"I should be there in about fifteen minutes. Wait for me, okay?"

"Wiseacre! I'm in no shape to walk more than a hundred feet."

"Be there soon. Bye." Dani got up from her desk and walked over to Max's office. She had noticed him look through his window at her, and assumed he had heard her phone chime.

"Dacque?" he asked.

"Yes. They sprung him, as he called it. I packed a bag lunch today. Would you mind if I picked him up, and then stayed for lunch with him? I will make sure I am back by one."

"That sounds like a great idea. He'll love that. Take your time, and I'll answer the phone until you return."

"Thanks Max."

Dacque was waiting in Room 222, in a wheelchair, when Dani arrived. It had taken her longer than she had guesstimated, but he was so happy to see her that he refrained from any wise comments. A nurse followed her into the room.

"He is all set to go, Miss. If you meet me there, I will wheel him down to the main door, and help you move him into your vehicle. He is much better today, and much happier, I must add."

Dani met the nurse at the main door and soon had Dacque loaded-up and on his way home. Dani was familiar with 7th Street, and his apartment complex, although she had never actually been inside. She found the closest parking spot she could to the back door, and helped him hobble to the elevator.

"Third floor," he advised. Fortunately, his apartment, 305 was not far from the elevator.

Dani helped Dacque over to the small kitchen table, with a chair at each end. "I packed a bag lunch. What can I make you for lunch?"

"I can make my own lunch, you know. I'm not disabled, just limping a bit."

"Sit. I have a surprise to share with you, and if we joust over who makes your lunch for too long, I won't have time to tell you until another day. What would you like?" she asked again, as she walked over and opened the refrigerator door.

"That's bribery, you know?" Dacque protested.

"Whatever works! What would you like?" The fridge was half full. Not bad for an elderly bachelor, Dani concluded.

"Toasted tomato and lettuce sounds pretty good."

Dani prepared the sandwich, and set it in front of him. "What would you like to drink?"

"Apple juice, please, if there is any left?"

Dani went back to the refrigerator, and picked up the can of apple juice. She swished it back and forth, gently, and figured there was probably one full glass remaining. She set the drink in front of Dacque, removed her sandwich from her purse, and sat down in the second chair.

Dacque never touched his sandwich, or his drink. He just sat there looking at Dani. "Well?"

"Well, what? Aren't you going to eat?"

"I let you make my lunch. You didn't say I had to eat it first. You promised me a surprise?"

Dani smiled. "There is nothing wrong with your memory, that's for sure."

"Fortunately I don't store it on my kneecap."

Dani roared. "You are really quick with your come backs, I must say."

"Skip the flattery and cut to the chase. Let's hear this big secret."

"Yes sir. Last night, a few minutes before eleven, Max phoned me again. Sara, his secretary, had just called him. Her father suffered a major heart attack, and she was catching the first flight available for Chicago. Max said she could be gone a few weeks, and asked if I would fill in for her until she returned."

"When do you start?"

"This morning."

"You were at Max's office when I called you? Why didn't you tell me about it then?"

"How could I force you to let me make your lunch, if the secret was out-of-the-bag too early?" Dani replied through a wide grin. "Now, eat your lunch. I told Max I would be back by one o'clock."

Chapter 9
The Plan

Happy to be home, Dacque abandoned his morning walk routine for a few days, allowing his wounded knee time to heal. Max had asked if Dani could work on Saturday, and she was delighted to receive an extra-day's pay that she had not anticipated. On Sunday, Dani picked up a few groceries for Dacque and spent part of the afternoon with him. Dani made it a habit to touch base with Dacque once or twice a day.

She would have loved to prepare him a home-cooked dinner, but could never be certain ahead of time whether Max would ask her to stay late, as he had on Monday and Tuesday. When she talked to Dacque on Tuesday evening she told him she would buy his favorite Chinese-food selections, and join him for dinner on Wednesday. The only catch was that she had no way of knowing if she would be asked once more to work extra hours, and that she was not prepared to say no to Max, so it could turn out to be a late dinner. Dacque assured her that he would be happy to devour his favorite Chinese-food dinner at midnight if necessary, so he would be ready whenever she arrived. Dani indicated that she would phone him when she was leaving work, so he would be forewarned.

Dani called Dacque on her cell phone, as she walked towards the parking garage on Lemon Avenue, and asked him to phone in their Chinese-food order so she could pick it up on the drive to his place. Fortunately, Max had declared, late in the afternoon, that he refused to work late three days in a row.

Chinese food in hand, Dani arrived at Dacque's apartment before six. They spread the containers out on the kitchen counter, and Dacque handed Dani a plate. "I'm not sure exactly what you ordered here," she said, "so you go first and that will give me a chance to check out my choices."

"You don't have to ask me twice," Dacque commented, and dug in.

It all looked pretty good to Dani so she decided to experiment with a little of everything, but was conservative with the helpings in case something did not taste as good as it looked. Dani joined Dacque at the table.

Appetites more than quenched, they chatted away across the table, with Dacque curious as to how she liked working for Max.

"He is a wonderful boss," Dani declared. "Nothing seems to faze him. He never gets angry if I make a mistake. I am so lucky that your accidental tumble introduced me to Max, and led to this brief respite from the unemployment line."

"There are no accidents." Dacque stated, matter-of-factly.

"Oh! So you want me to believe that you deliberately dived, face first into the pavement in front of a spiffily-dressed lawyer so he could provide me with a temporary legal secretary position, when his secretary's father thought it was a convenient time to have a major heart attack? Give me a break."

"It was all part of a plan."

"Sometimes, Dacque, I think you are just plain nuts," Dani declared, her voice rising noticeably. "What plan?"

"I know it is difficult to accept, but let me give you my take on all of this?" Dacque responded, unfazed.

"Let's hear it. This better be good!"

"God would know that Sara's father was about to have a heart attack. God would know when Max was on his way to his office. How long were you sitting on the bench in MacDunnah Park that first day we met, before I surprised you?"

"Probably fifteen to twenty minutes."

"And on the second day when you went there to see if I would return?"

"I would say probably about the same amount of time."

"God led me to MacDunnah Park the first day, I believe, and when I walked by and tried to ignore this sobbing young lady on the park bench, I was ordered to go back to you. On the second morning, I started to walk south, not north, and was distinctly told I was going the wrong way. I was once again led back to the Park where you were waiting for me. Waiting for me! Those were not accidents. There is a plan unfolding here, one that has required me to put you in touch with Max. I really have no idea why, but without a doubt, we will eventually find out."

"What about your swan-dive onto the sidewalk?"

"I guess God had to think of something to attract Max's attention."

"If you and God are such good buddies, why did He bang up your knee so much?"

"Well, if I was not hurt, and Max just helped me to my feet and we both went on our merry way, then you two would have never met, right?"

Dani sighed. Dacque made it sound so plausible it was difficult to argue with him. If God sends him messages, she reasoned, then why could He not set all of these events in motion. A plan! Who would have imagined it?

Chapter 10
Edgar Cayce

Dani and Dacque settled their over-stuffed bodies into more comfortable chairs in Dacque's living room, after carefully transferring the Chinese-food leftovers to Dacque's refrigerator.

Amazed and bewildered, by Dacque's nonchalant declaration that the events of the past couple of weeks were all part of a plan being orchestrated by God, Dani decided that there was no better time than the present to inquire just how it came about that Dacque and the Heavenly Powers became so intimate. "Dacque," she said cautiously, "please try to fill me in, in terms that I can understand, on what you call the plan, how your connection to God works, and for that matter, how it came about?"

Dacque smiled. "I would be delighted to! It may take a while."

"I've got all evening, if you have?"

"I have too," Dacque replied, and commenced his oratory. "It did not just happen, but evolved over a number of years. Before I retired, my life was pretty-much centered on my family, my career, and a few hobbies here-and-there. Then, after I retired, I found I had time on my hands, a situation I was basically unaccustomed to and unprepared for. I had always been interested in biographies, but because my teaching job required a lot of reading and preparation, I did a minimal amount of recreational reading.

"My late wife loved to visit yard sales and flea markets, looking for undiscovered treasures, and I would often accompany her and snoop through the used books, picking up one here-and-there, that piqued my interest. Most were biographies of famous politicians, actors, musicians, sports heroes, and such. One day I found a biography of an interesting American that I had never even heard of. His name was Edgar Cayce. Have you ever heard of him?"

"No, I can't say that I have," Dani replied.

"I'm not surprised. He passed on in 1945, long before you were even born, but he is regarded today as America's legendary mystic."

"What's a mystic?" Dani interrupted.

"That's a good question, and I'm not positive that I completely understand it myself. My definition would be an individual, who would be considered psychic by many, and who has an innate understanding of and connection with the God Force."

"Like you?"

Dacque laughed. "I definitely do not consider myself a mystic, but if I am, I would be on the bottom rung of a very tall ladder, and Edgar Cayce would be on the top rung. Before you leave this evening, make sure that I remember to send along with you a copy of the book that introduced me to Edgar Cayce in the first place. It is called, There Is a River, by Thomas Sugrue. It is the only biography of Edgar Cayce that was published before his death in 1945. There have been at least thirty others published since his death. Try counting on your fingers the number of people who might have had over thirty biographies published about them."

Dani silently counted on her fingers for a minute before giving up. "Not very many, that I can think of."

Dacque continued the story of his awakening. "Edgar Cayce was born in rural Kentucky, but in his middle years was guided to settle in a coastal fishing village in Virginia, called Virginia Beach. Over his lifetime, he gave more than fifteen thousand psychic readings in a self-induced, coma-like, trance state. Copies of over fourteen thousand of these readings have been preserved in the archives of his Association for Research and Enlightenment, or A.R.E. About ten thousand of these readings were medical readings, where in his unconscious state he was able to diagnose problems that medical doctors in those days could not locate or identify, and even prescribed medical procedures and medicines that had not yet been invented.

"The next largest group-of-readings is reincarnation or past life readings, some 2500 readings for about 2000 different individuals. Edgar Cayce was a very religious person, as well as a Sunday-School teacher, and he was personally disturbed when the first reading implying reincarnation surfaced. A careful search of the Scriptures convinced him that there was actually nothing in the Bible that contradicted the notion of reincarnation, and in fact, a number of verses that pretty-much, if read with an open mind, implied that reincarnation existed. Convinced that reincarnation was at least possible, Edgar and a group of friends commenced a series of readings seeking an explanation of this unknown world that many people today still do not believe exists. This initial investigation, over many decades, led to an enormous number of readings that revealed previous incarnations back to Atlantis and Adam, and to Creation."

Dani stared at Dacque glassy-eyed, as if in a stupor, but said nothing. Dacque deduced that it was probably the appropriate time to recess the story of his awakening, give her some material to read, and let her slowly digest all of the information. When, or if, she was ready, he would continue the story of his own miraculous discoveries.

Dacque stood up. "I have something that I would like to show you on the computer," he told Dani as he walked towards his laptop on the dining room table, "and while the computer is warming-up, I will get you that Edgar Cayce biography that I mentioned."

Dacque activated the laptop and then disappeared behind a closed door, returning seconds later with a book in-hand.

"Before you read this, I would suggest that you read some articles on Edgar Cayce that appeared a few years ago in magazines and on the internet, by a Canadian writer by the name of Doug Simpson. I cannot tell you much about him, but his articles make informative reading. Have you got your notepad in your purse?"

"Yes," Dani responded. "I'll grab it."

She joined Dacque at the dining room table, positioning herself behind him so that she could see the computer screen, just as a new website popped up.

"Have you got your notepad?"

"Yes."

"His website is at dousimp.mnsi.net. When you go there, I recommend that you read a few articles in this particular order. First, Edgar Cayce's Earliest Psychic Readings, gives you an interesting look at how he first discovered his unusual abilities. Next, go to Edgar Cayce's First Miracle Reading. It describes the reading which was probably the most influential in convincing him that his life was destined to be devoted to helping others, with God's assistance. The third one, Edgar Cayce Becomes a National Celebrity, is rather self-explanatory. After those three, I suggest that you then turn to some of his reincarnation articles, like Martha Washington, Thomas Jefferson, Elizabeth, The Mother of John the Baptist, Mary Magdalene, and one called Who Were You In Your Past Lifetimes? Doug does not actually publish his articles on his website, he instead sends visitors to his site to the actual websites and magazines where his articles have been published in six different countries."

Dacque stood up and turned to face Dani. "After you have had a chance to read and digest those articles, and any others that you might want to look at while you are there, then you are probably ready to begin reading, There Is a River. If you have any questions, at any time, please call me. I know that I have only started to tell you my story, but this Edgar Cayce material will help you accept my experiences and hopefully convince you that I'm not 'just plain nuts' as you suggested earlier."

Dani cracked a grin and her eyes started to water. She quickly took Dacque in her arms and clung tightly to him. "I'm sorry," she whispered in his ear, "but I feel like I'm afloat in the middle of the ocean. Please forgive me."

Chapter 11
Oliver

Late on Friday afternoon, Max returned from one of his numerous jaunts to other areas of the law firm's offices and stopped in front of Dani's desk. "The firm is a sponsor of the Anywhere Arts and Entertainment Center and has eight season tickets to all of their events, which all employees may use. There were three tickets left for tomorrow night's musical production of Oliver," he explained to Dani, "so I asked for them. I suspect that, on your first day, Payroll advised you of the firm's policy on employees of the firm not dating each other, so, would you like to go to the production, as a fellow employee?"

"That would be wonderful!" Dani replied.

"I would be happy to pick you up, if you like, or we can meet there? I am not taking a date, so there is one extra ticket which you can use if you would like to bring along a boyfriend, or girlfriend, or whoever. Do you think that Dacque might be interested?"

"I do not have a boyfriend, or even a girlfriend to bring, but I could ask Dacque if he is interested in going," Dani advised.

Max handed Dani two of the tickets. "You can let me know tomorrow if you would like me to pick you up, or the two of you, otherwise, I will see you there."

"Thank you, Max. I will let you know either way."

***

Dani and Dacque entered the auditorium, and Dani handed their tickets to an usher. Dacque had been delighted to accept Dani's invitation to use the extra ticket, and she had called Max to advise him that she would drive Dacque to the Center and they would meet him there. The usher stopped a few rows from the front of the auditorium, and returned the tickets. "There you go, Miss, F1 and 2, right on the aisle."

"Thank, you!" Dani replied, as she noticed a smiling Max stand up to greet them.

"I was beginning to wonder if you were going to make it before the show got started, but you obviously did. Dacque, you look much, much better than the last time I saw you. How is the knee?" he asked, extending his hand.

"Almost as good as new," Dacque replied, shaking Max's hand. "The tumble definitely could have been much worse. Thank you for thinking of me for your extra ticket, and, of course, all of your efforts and concern on the day of my tumble."

The auditorium lights dimmed, and Dacque guided Dani in beside Max before settling into the aisle seat.

***

Max walked, with Dani and Dacque, to the parking lot after the conclusion of a marvelous production. They all took turns praising the performance. "Anyone care for a drink or a bite to eat?" Max asked. "My treat."

Dani looked at Dacque, but figured she knew what his response would be. "It's up to you?"

"To be perfectly honest, I am rather tired, but thank you so much for the offer, and for a wonderful evening. I thoroughly enjoyed myself," Dacque replied, extending a hand to Max.

"You are most welcome."

"Yes, thanks for everything, Max," Dani chimed in, and walked Dacque, arm and arm, to her car.

Chapter 12
Pleasant Surprise

Wednesday afternoon, Dani was working away at her computer when Max opened his office door and called to her. "Dani, could you come in here, please?"

Dani picked up her stenographers' pad and joined Max in his office. Max re-closed the door. "I have Barb Bradford on the line. She is the Bradford in the law firm of Williams, Bradford and Williams. Are you familiar with them?"

"I've heard of them, but that's about all I know."

"They specialize in personal injury claims. I have known her for almost twenty years; I went to high school and later law school with her younger brother, Ben Jr. It is a father-daughter-son law firm. I played basketball last night at the gym with Ben Jr. and he happened to mention that Barb's secretary was retiring at the end of the month. I jumped right in and recommended you to Ben, on the spot, and he said he would pass the info on to Barb. They were getting ready to advertise the opening soon, but after the glowing report I gave you, Barb would like to talk to you."

Dani's eyes lit up. "Wow!"

"Come on over and settle into the boss' chair and I will take a break while you two have a chat. I advised her that you could leave work, if necessary, and go for an interview, at a time that was convenient for her."

***

When Max returned to his office, Dani was, once again, working away on her computer. He could tell by the smile on her face that the conversation had gone well. "What's the news?"

"I have an interview at her office at five-thirty today. Thank you so much for using your influence in all of this. If I happen to get the position, could that cause a problem for you? I certainly don't want to do that."

"I suspect Sara will be back before the end of the month, but if she isn't, then I will just call-in a temp. Do not miss out on a permanent position worrying about me. Do you hear me, young lady?"

"Yes, yes. Thank you so much for everything, Max."

Chapter 13
Soul Awakening

Dani left the offices of Williams, Bradford and Williams, literally dancing-on-air. Her interview with Barb Bradford had gone impeccably. Barb was impressed with her resume and their personalities had clicked, immediately. Barb hired her on the spot. It was past six-thirty as Dani walked towards her parked car. She called Dacque.

"Hello."

"Hello, Dacque. Sorry I'm late but something came up. I'll tell you all about it when I get there. Call in the Chinese-food order, and I will pick it up."

"I'm on it."

Dani and Dacque carried their heaping dinner plates to Dacque's kitchen table, and sat down. Dani was starving and commenced to dig-in, instantly, but Dacque left his fork on the table and patiently stared at her.

"Aren't you hungry?" she asked, but immediately realized that her excitement over the earlier events must have been obvious to her new friend. "Are you psychic, like Edgar Cayce?" she asked.

"One doesn't have to be psychic to read the excitement in your face. Out with it!" he demanded.

"I just came from a job interview that Max set up with another law firm where he has long-standing connections. They hired me on the spot. Can you believe it?"

"Of course! It is all part of the plan," Dacque replied, "but I'm really thrilled about it, too. Congratulations."

"Thank you." Dani was about to make a derogatory remark about Dacque's 'plan', but was grateful that she caught herself before she did so. All of the dominoes in her life had been miraculously falling into place since she had met Dacque that day at MacDunnah Park. It was becoming more and more difficult, as time passed, for her to deny that there was some unseen force manipulating the recent events in her life.

After dinner, they lounged in the living room. All week, neither of them had mentioned their discussion from the previous Wednesday about the Edgar Cayce readings. "I read the articles," Dani informed Dacque, "that you showed me last week on your computer, about how Edgar Cayce discovered his unimaginable powers, and also the ones on the reincarnation of souls. The whole idea is mind-boggling, yet it does make sense in some ways. I started reading the book, There Is a River, but I am not that far along. What I would like to hear about next is your understanding of souls and reincarnation, in simple terms that I can understand, okay?"

"Okay," Dacque replied. "My initial understanding came from the Edgar Cayce material, but I have also researched other sources. Sometimes one source contradicts information from another source, so we have to try and figure out which version makes more sense to us. Also, keep in mind that there is no real proof, in most cases, of what we read, just like there is no real proof of the existence of God. It basically boils down to believing it on faith, if it makes sense to each one of us."

"I understand," Dani acknowledged.

"Apparently, after God Created the Universes, and directed the evolution of the Earth in particular, it was a marvelously beautiful place, with all sorts of animals, birds, and other creatures enjoying their environment. Man did not exist then, and was not even in God's plan. At some point God felt lonely and wanted to share these beautiful surroundings with others.

"Don't think of God as resembling humans, but more like an enormous field of energy with the ability to think. Apparently, God caused an explosion of some nature within His energy field, and all of the souls were created at the same time by God and from God. Thus, all souls could be considered sons and daughters of God, and brothers and sisters. After you grasp that idea, I need to shake it up on you. Souls are actually sexless, neither male nor female; it is the bodies that they inhabit that are male and female. Apparently, most of our souls have already done so, or in some future incarnation will inhabit male as well as female bodies, and will experience many or all of the different races. There is a very important lesson to be learned here. People who dislike, make fun of, or deliberately harm individuals of a particular race, are creating bad Karma, and in some future incarnation will be required to incarnate in that particular race and suffer in some similar fashion to the suffering caused. The eye for an eye moral is real.

"At least one soul, the soul of Jesus, has always incarnated as a male. The Immaculate Conception of Mary did occur as indicated in the Bible. The soul of Jesus had a number of previous incarnations, but that story definitely must wait for another time.

"Apparently, souls are on an educational journey to become God-Like, as they were originally, and part of that educational process involves incarnating in human bodies. When a soul has experienced or learned the proper lessons, it may remain with God, and not need to reincarnate again, but it can also do so if desired, often to be of assistance to another incarnated soul with whom it experienced a previous incarnation.

"Before the Creation of man, and yes I said Creation not evolution, souls, as a former part of God were a thinking energy, and some of them strayed from God's intended path, but not all of them. Apparently there are some God-Like souls that have never incarnated, and these souls may be what we refer to as Angels."

Dacque paused, and waited for a reaction. Dani appeared to be in a state of shock or hypnosis. "Are you alright?" he asked.

"I have no idea. That was one mind-boggling explanation. I'm not even going to attempt to ask a question right now. I need to think this whole concept through for a while, and may eventually come back with questions, sometime."

"May I make a suggestion?" Dacque asked.

"Of course."

"Are you still saying your prayers each night until you fall asleep?"

"Yes. Why?"

"In your prayers, add the request for an understanding of the Creation and reincarnation of souls, and don't be surprised if your understanding gradually improves."

"I will do that."

Chapter 14
Changing Times

Friday morning, as Dani entered Max's outer-office, he waved at her to come into his office and closed the door. He was not his usually-jovial self. She had telephoned Max on Wednesday evening, after she returned home from her Chinese-food dinner and educational chat at Dacque's apartment, and had informed him of the good news concerning her interview with Barb Bradford. He had been delighted. She said a quick, silent prayer, 'Please, Lord, don't let me lose my new job. Amen.' "Is everything alright?" she asked.

"Basically, yes," Max replied. "Sara called me last night and said that her father's condition has now stabilized and he was doing well, so she would be flying home this weekend and returning to work on Monday. I want to update the office staff today, but felt that you deserved to be the first to know."

"Thank you for that. I am glad to hear that Sara's father is doing well. You and I both knew that my employment here was for a very short term, and I will be eternally grateful for the time I spent here. Not only did I replenish my bank account, but, thanks to your connections, I am leaving with a permanent job that will commence in two weeks. I must admit that it will be sad not to be here every morning, but I would not have missed these past two-and-a-half weeks for anything. Now smile. Don't look so glum."

Max flashed a wide grin. "I hated to have to tell you, but I had no other option. I thought you might get another week here, but it wasn't meant to be. I will definitely miss having you around. Your vivacious personality has brightened up these sometimes sterile premises."

"Thank you. Shall I get to work, before I get fired on my last day?"

Max laughed this time. "I don't think we have to worry about that."

***

A few minutes before four o'clock, Max zipped out of his office, in an obvious hurry, and paused in front of Dani's desk. "I wanted to be here to say goodbye at the end of the day, but I need to leave the office to put out a bit of an emergency-fire, and it is not likely that I will get back quickly. I'm sorry about that. If you don't mind, I will phone you later tonight?"

"I will look forward to that," Dani replied, and Max hurried out the office door.

Chapter 15
Late Night Phone Call

Dani was reading Thomas Sugrue's, There Is a River, when her cell phone chimed. "Hello."

"Hello Dani. It's Max. I hope I'm not calling too late?"

"Not a problem. I was doing some reading before bedtime. Did you dowse your fire this afternoon?"

"It wasn't a big deal. The client was unable to find an item in a proposal, so it was a big deal to him. I am sincerely sorry that I was not there to say goodbye when you left. I feel bad about that," Max added.

"Don't feel bad. You could not avoid it. I'm sure we will see each other around, now and then."

"I'm sure we will." There was a momentary pause before Max continued. "Actually, I was wondering, now that we are no longer employed at the same firm, could I interest you in going out with me on a real date tomorrow night?"

Dani was caught off guard, but then again, she was not. Max had always been a perfect gentleman around her, but at times, when they had looked into each other's eyes, she had thought she detected a sparkle of non-employer interest. "Well, I think there is a possibility that could happen, but a very wise lawyer once told me that a good proposal must always include all of the details."

"He was a wise fellow. Anyone I know?"

"Actually, you meet him every morning in the bathroom mirror."

"Oh! Him! He never talks to me."

"Maybe that's just as well," Dani shot back.

"I guess we need to commence the negotiation process," Max said, moving on to the business at hand. "I had in mind a nice dinner, somewhere, and then possibly a movie, or maybe a dance club, if you like to dance? I should warn you right off the bat that I am not a great dancer. A third option could be some other activity which might be more up your line. All I really know about your non-office interests is that you like to walk. Anything there sound interesting?"

"I think I detect the groundwork for an eventual agreement here," Dani replied. "I consider myself just an average Joe. I guess that should be Joanne. To be perfectly truthful, I would feel somewhat out-of-place in a real ritzy restaurant. I'm more of a Momma's home cooking, casual kind of gal."

"I know just the place. Have you ever been to Kathy's Kitchen?"

"No. I can't say that I have even heard of it."

"It is a wonderful little place. I go in there two or three times a week for a late dinner, on my way home from the office. I am not much of a cook. To be truthful, I don't cook. I can make a sandwich, or open a can and put something in the microwave, but when I want a real meal then I drop into Kathy's."

"Sounds like we have dinner settled," Dani responded. "Do you have any movies or dance clubs in mind?"

"If you want the truth? No. I don't do either very often. Do you have any ideas?"

"I have not been paying any attention to the movies that are playing, and seldom go myself. I also do not enjoy the loud dance clubs that the younger crowd seems to prefer today, but I have been a few times to an out-of-the-way nightclub, where they have a small combo playing much quieter and slower music."

"Sounds perfect to this fellow. Do we have all of the details negotiated?" Max asked.

"Can I assume we are talking casual dress? I have never seen you in anything but a suit and tie."

"Part of the show. Part of the show. It never takes me very long to climb out of them when I get home, believe me. Inside, I too am more of a casual guy, as well. Casual wear it is. How about I pick you up at five?"

"I'll be ready."

"Swell. Goodnight Dani."

"Do you have my address?"

"That would certainly come in handy."

Dani gave him her address. "See you tomorrow."

Chapter 16
Walking Partners

Dani was up early on Saturday morning, refreshed by a good night's sleep and looking forward to the evening's date with Max. It felt like a perfect morning for a walk, an activity that she had abandoned entirely after Dacque's tumble and her temporary employment with Max's law firm. As eight-fifteen rolled around, she reasoned that Dacque should be up, yet would not likely have left on his walk, so she called him.

"Hello."

"Hello Dacque. It's Dani. Are you going for your walk this morning?"

"Yes, Around nine."

"I could use a good walk. Mind if I meet you some place?"

There was more than a moments silence on the other end of the line. "I have a better idea. Why don't you drive over here, and we can start off together? That way you will get a chance to see how my walks are directed by the stop-lights."

"Okay, I'll be there by nine."

Dani was waiting in the foyer when Dacque exited the elevator.

"Would you like to go north or south this morning?" he asked Dani.

"Which way would you go if I wasn't here?"

"It should be a north day," Dacque replied.

"North it is."

They entered the bright sunshine, and turned north on 7th Street. The stoplight at Olive Avenue turned yellow as they approached the corner. "Would you like to cross 7th Street on the green, or turn right and walk along Olive to the east?"

"You pick," Dani said.

"No, today you get to make the decisions. Let's see where we end up."

"Okay, let's cross 7th Street, and go west."

They walked west along Olive, and caught a green light at 9th Street, but a red at 10th Street. "Shall we go left, or cross Olive on the green and go north?" Dacque asked.

Dani looked across Olive Street at the familiar surroundings, and crossed with the light.

They entered MacDunnah Park and walked north on the East Path. "That is exactly the route I was led to follow that first morning when I encountered you on the bench in tears," Dacque said.

"Do you think we were led here again for a reason?" Dani asked.

"I really don't know. I haven't heard any voices, today, but let's stop and sit on our bench for a few minutes, and see what happens, if anything."

The morning walkers settled down on the bench where they had met two days in a row a few weeks previously. Neither spoke, as they watched the birds swoop back and forth and the squirrels play tag. Ten minutes passed in silence, before Dacque turned to Dani. "What is it you are thinking about asking me, but are not sure you should, today?"

"How did you know that?"

"I was told to ask you what it is that you wanted to ask me, as you are ready for the answer."

"Amazing!" Dani exclaimed. "Downright amazing!"

"Ask your question."

Dani hesitated a few seconds, but quickly deduced that it must be in the plan. "Do you know anything about your past lifetimes?"

"Oh, yes, I have info on about a dozen of them."

"How did you learn about them?" she asked.

It was Dacque's turn to hesitate. He would not have presumed that she was ready for this conversation, but apparently the Powers-That-Be, knew otherwise. "There is a small number of us, around the Anywhere area, that are part of a Reincarnation Enlightenment Group. We meet every couple of months, and also communicate by email in-between. We only know each other's alias or group name, and communicate between meetings through special email addresses that we have set up exclusively for this purpose, not through our regular email accounts.

"There is a young woman, probably a few years older than you, who is a certified hypnotherapist. By day, she works with individuals who seek help for medical or mental problems, like stopping smoking or fears of things like high places or drowning. In some of her hypnotic sessions, over the years, patients had skipped back into past lifetimes, so she decided that she would like to investigate the topic further. She was one of the founding members of our group. I did not discover them until a year or two later. As part of her research, this lady will use hypnosis to regress group members into past lifetimes, for free, during her non-working hours. I have had three regression sessions with her, where I discovered at least some of my past lifetimes."

"Tell me about them, will you?"

"No, at least not yet," Dacque replied.

"Why not?"

"Just in case you, or others, might decide that sometime in the future you would like to join our group and have some regression sessions, the group members have agreed not to openly share their past lifetimes with each other. Because there is a possibility that group members, who in-effect have found each other in this lifetime, or were led to each other like we were, may have experienced previous lifetimes together, we have agreed to not share our past-lifetime history, under normal circumstances."

"Normal circumstances?"

"At our bimonthly meetings, now and then, or through emails, an individual may be specifically seeking others who shared a particular lifetime with him or her, and may ask a question such as, 'I have had a past lifetime in France in the sixteenth century. If anyone else here has also had a French incarnation around that time period, I would appreciate it if we could share names and general information from those experiences, and see if we might have known each other back then.' Those who are willing to share, can agree to meet and share their information, or do it online, but the other group members will not be invited to take part.

"It is generally believed to be important that members, in particular those who have not uncovered a fair number of past incarnations, not be placed in a position where they might consciously desire to have had an incarnation with another individual or maybe in the same time period, and this strong desire might lodge in their subconscious mind and later appear as a past lifetime, when it, in effect, is not reality, but only a desire.

"For example, if you knew that I had an incarnation as a senator in Rome with Julius Caesar, and you got it into your mind that you would love to have had an incarnation as a senator with Julius Caesar, it is possible, rare but possible, that your subconscious mind could manufacture an incarnation that was not real based on your soul's knowledge of the times of Julius Caesar, but just wished for. Apparently, our subconscious minds remember everything, not just actions and words but also thoughts, from all of our past lifetimes.

"You and I were drawn together, you must admit in a most unusual manner, so that it would not surprise me if our meeting was orchestrated because we had a previous lifetime together and still have some unfinished business to be addressed. If you ever get to the point where you know of approximately ten previous incarnations, then comparing our past lifetimes for incarnations together makes sense. It is generally believed that the past incarnations, which we uncover in this lifetime, are not the most historical ones but the more significant ones related to our purpose for being here on earth in this lifetime. So, after you have discovered ten or twelve previous incarnations, it is much-less-likely that your subconscious mind would manufacture a past lifetime based solely on desires."

"Wow! Complicated, very complicated, but I think I understand the concept," Dani said. "Let's continue our walk. I have lots to think about"

Chapter 17
First Date

Dani, not one to subscribe to the notion of fashionably late, was dressed and ready-to-go well before five o'clock. She was wearing her favorite pair of black slacks and the non-revealing bright-red blouse that she had specifically purchased, a while back, to contrast with the black slacks. At four-fifty, she tossed a dressy, white jacket over her arm, and decided to ride down and wait for Max in the foyer, outside of the elevator.

Max opened the right-hand door to the apartment building, and appeared somewhat startled as Dani unexpectedly hopped to her feet from a sofa in the foyer to the right of the door. Max stared at her for a long moment. "That is one attention-demanding outfit," he declared. "I love it."

"Thank you. I was all ready and waiting, early, so I decided to save you some time and searching, and came down here."

"That's fine by me," Max stated, and held open the door for her.

Dani noticed that the only vehicle in visitors parking was a sparkling, off-white Cadillac. In the two-and-a-half weeks that she had worked for Max, she had never seen him in a vehicle, so she was unaware of exactly what his car of choice was.

Max opened the passenger door for her, and Dani eased herself onto the white leather seat. She could not recall ever being in a car this luxurious in her entire life. "Very nice car," she commented as Max climbed into the seat beside her.

"Thank you. It's part of the show. Most of my clients are multimillionaires who are accustomed to being driven around in limousines. I'm not in their league, but this is a reasonable substitute, on my income."

Max drove east on Pineapple Avenue and turned south on Main Street. It took them a while to get through the center of the city at that hour. Kathy's Kitchen was located in a newer strip-mall on the southern extremity of Anywhere.

"Hello, Max," a fiftyish-looking waitress greeted him, enthusiastically, as they entered the restaurant. "And look at this lovely lady you have with you this evening. I just adore your outfit, dear."

"Kathy, this is Dani. Dani, this is Kathy, the best cook in Anywhere," Max said.

"He's lying to you, dear. My husband may be the best cook in Anywhere, but my job is to blarney the customers. Max loves attention, in case you haven't noticed?"

"I'll try to remember that," Dani replied, as Max led her to a booth at the rear of the surprisingly-small restaurant.

Kathy brought them menus and glasses of water, and retreated to allow them time to make their selections.

Dani noticed the hot-turkey sandwich, with peas, mashed potatoes and gravy. "I haven't had one of those in ages," she said to Max.

"They are one of my favorites. I make sure I order at least one a week," Max advised her.

They both devoured hot-turkey sandwiches. "Do you have room for desert?" Kathy asked on one of her visits.

"Nothing for me, thank you," Dani replied. "I am stuffed. You go ahead, Max, if you have room."

Max loved Kathy's pies, but politely declined. They sat in their booth for a while longer, sipping coffee and making small-talk. It was much too early to head for the night club that Dani had recommended, so Max suggested that they drive over to the new, indoor mall, a mile further south on Main Street.

They cruised around the mall, which Dani had only been to once before, and stopped here and there. Dani tried on some shoes that were on sale at one of the stores, but, in the end, decided against purchasing any.

When some of the establishments began to close-up for the evening, Max and Dani departed from the mall and commenced the rather long journey to the north end of the city where Dani's favorite night-spot was located. It was called The Basement Hide-A-Way, appropriately named for its location in the basement of an old factory, which had been renovated into unique shops and art studios.

It was after nine-thirty before they entered the Hide-A-Way. It was dimly-lit, and had a handful of patrons, but, right-away, Max was pleased when he heard the quiet tune that the three-piece- combo was bringing to life. Dani led them to a table near the back wall. When the waiter arrived, she ordered a Peña Colada and Max settled for a draft beer. They chatted and enjoyed the music for a while, until the combo started in with Hey Jude. "That's one of my favorite songs," Dani declared, holding out her hand to Max. "Come. Dance with me?"

For the next two hours they alternated their time between listening and dancing. Dani felt so relaxed and secure with their bodies almost glued together as one, and barely swaying back and forth to the soothing music, that she apparently dozed off momentarily and might have ended up on the floor if not for Max's bear-hug around her waist. "Are you alright?"

"I guess I actually fell asleep, didn't I?"

"I suspect so. I think it's time to go," Max suggested.

Max pulled the Cadillac to a stop in front of the entrance to Dani's apartment building. "Would you like to come in for a while? It's not that late, and I'm awake now," Dani said.

Max moved the car into visitors parking, and they proceeded inside.

After unlocking her apartment door, Dani flicked on the light and turned the dead-bolt. "Make yourself at home for a couple of minutes," she instructed Max. "I need to make a pit stop."

On the way past her CD player, she pushed the on button, and Anne Murray commenced to croon.

Max slowly surveyed the living area of Dani's apparently small apartment with its mix-and-match furnishings. "Obviously, a working-girl's abode," he said quietly to himself. He had spent most of his life living in similar accommodations, so his perception was backed up by decades of experience. As he sat down on one end of the sofa, he noticed a paperback book on the end table and picked it up. There Is a River, by Thomas Sugrue, the cover said. "Never heard of him," Max again said, talking to himself, and placed the book back where he had found it.

Dani returned to the room. "Can I get you a drink, or a snack?" she offered.

"No thanks, I'm good."

"Anne Murray has some great songs on that CD. Would you like to dance some more or just sit and chat?" she asked.

"Dancing is fine with me," Max responded, and stood up. They swayed through the remainder of the songs on the CD, and were jolted alert by the silence. "I should probably be on my way," Max said to Dani, leaning his head forward and kissing her momentarily on her up-stretched lips.

"Is that the best you can do?" she whispered.

The passionate embrace that ensued ignited too-long-dormant hormonal explosions, culminating with Max sweeping Dani off of her feet, and carrying her down the hallway. "I believe thou seekest the door on the left, Sir Gallant Knight," Dani whispered in his ear.

Chapter 18
Unexplained Attraction

Dani and Max slept-in late on Sunday morning. After Dani cooked him a hefty, bacon and egg breakfast, Max left her apartment to return home for a shower, to be followed by a quiet afternoon's work at his law office on a merger proposal.

After a refreshing shower of her own, Dani logged onto the computer and continued her research into reincarnation. She decided on her code name or alias, to be used as a member of the Reincarnation Enlightenment Group, and signed up for another email account to be used solely for that purpose, as required by the group. She checked to see if the Group had a website, but could not find one. It appeared, to her, that all of their communications were carried out on a personal basis.

When the morning rains had apparently concluded, and the sun brightened up a dreary day, she called Dacque to see if he had gone for his morning walk, showers or no showers, or was waiting for the weather to clear. He advised her that he had postponed his morning walk, and was preparing to leave when the phone rang. Dani joined him on his walk, and told him all about her wonderful first date with Max, discretely ending her story at the point when Max drove her home from The Basement Hide-A-Way. She gave him her reincarnation-group alias and new email address, and Dacque said that he would submit it to the group leader, the certified hypnotist, with his recommendation that she be welcomed into the group.

With all of that accomplished, Dani had time on her hands. She tried to read, There Is a River, but her mind continually wandered back to her evening and night with Max. All outward signs seemed to indicate that he truly liked her, but she had a gnawing dread that she might just be another conquest, another notch in his gun, and that she would never hear from him again.

She put the book down and stretched out on the sofa, opting to veg in front of the television set.

Dani sensed a habitual ringing sound, and jolted awake when she realized it was the chime on her cell phone. When she checked the caller ID, she was relieved. "Hi, Max. How did you make out at the office today?"

"Truthfully, progress was slow. My mind kept wandering back to our time together, recently."

Dani smiled to herself. That was definitely a good omen. "Well, I guess if I have such a detrimental effect on your work, we will have to avoid each other in the future." she teased.

"A snowball's chance in Florida that will happen!" he declared. "At this point in time, I can't put my finger on it, but I have this magnetic attraction to you. Don't get me wrong, here, I know you are a lovely young lady with a wonderful personality, but there is something more to it that I cannot find an explanation for."

"A girl must retain an air of mystery about herself, just to keep her suitors off-beat."

"So I've heard," Max retorted, "although I'm not sure that's it either."

"I guess you'll just have to work on it, until you figure it out. Are you still at the office?"

"No, I left about an hour ago, had dinner at Kathy's, and then I came home."

"It's not that late. How about coming over and visiting me? You can work on your unexplained-magnetism problem, maybe, but I do not suspect that we will spend a lot of time in conversation."

The line fell silent for a few seconds, as Max translated the meaning of her words. "I'm on my way."

Chapter 19
Biding Time

Dani walked with Dacque every morning, at approximately nine o'clock. She had no illusions about continuing this enjoyable routine after she started working at Williams, Bradford and Williams, but she was determined to maximize her exercise time while she had the opportunity.

During their Monday-morning walk, Dacque advised her that he had emailed her request for membership in the Reincarnation Enlightenment Group, along with his recommendation, on Sunday afternoon. He said that she would likely receive an email back, within a few days, and to keep checking her new email account daily.

Wednesday evening, before Max arrived for his now-regular evening visit, Dani noticed the anticipated email:

Dear Beanpole,
Your request for membership in the Reincarnation Enlightenment Group, submitted on your behalf by Streetwalker, has been granted. Welcome! When you attend your first group meeting, you will receive your name tag, and we request that you wear it to all meetings.

Some members, like you and Streetwalker, are aware of the identity of other members, but I wish to impress upon you the necessity of maintaining identity secrecy, and hope that you will take extra care to prevent yourself from accidently using the name you call Streetwalker in other circumstances, while attending our group meetings.

The attached file contains the group name and group email for all members, for your use in appropriate communications. An email has also been sent to all other members advising them of your group name and email. Please contact me immediately if you receive inappropriate emails. This has not been a problem in the past, but if the situation does arise in the future, we will address it forth-with.

Once again, welcome to the Reincarnation Enlightenment Group.

Eyeonthepast

Dani signed out of her new account, as she anticipated Max would be arriving before long. Of course, Max knew nothing about her and Dacque's interest in reincarnation and past lives, and she planned to keep it that way, at least for the foreseeable future.

Chapter 20
Making Contact

Dani ushered Max out of her apartment, following another passionate embrace. It was so tempting to climb back into bed and dream sweet dreams, but, time was of the essence. She reactivated her computer and signed-in to her new email account.

Dear Eyeonthepast,
Thank you for your email, and for accepting me as a member of the Reincarnation Enlightenment Group.

My friend, Streetwalker, advised me that you performed past-life regressions for group members, in your spare time. It probably will not come as a great surprise when I tell you that I am very interested in discovering some of my past lifetimes. Streetwalker explained that because I was recommended for membership by a member in good standing, then it might be possible for me to schedule a past-life regression session with you, at your convenience, before I attend my first group meeting. Streetwalker has told me that he has uncovered a number of his past lives during three regression sessions with you, and he also explained why he could not tell me anything about them. I cannot wait to discover mine!

I am currently between jobs, but on the first of the month will begin new employment, steady days, which can involve some overtime after

5:00, in emergencies. I also have a new boyfriend, who works a lot of overtime into the evening and on weekends, so I try to reserve time to spend with him after nine in the evening. My point to all of this is that I normally have free time between five and nine on weekdays, and afternoons on the weekend, which, according to Streetwalker, are the times when you usually hold your regression sessions for members. My cell-phone number is 555-456-7890, and I would greatly appreciate hearing from you if you can find time in your busy schedule for me, at your convenience.

Sincerely

Beanpole

Chapter 21
Reliving Past Lives

Dani nervously awaited the arrival of Eyeonthepast for their one o'clock appointment. She had calculated, when Eye had telephoned her on Thursday evening, that she could maneuver her Saturday afternoon schedule around the one-to-four timeslot. Max had spent the night, as she speculated he would, and departed before ten for an afternoon of legal work, but would return at five for their second Saturday evening of dinner and dancing. If Max had not stayed overnight, she would have accompanied Dacque on his morning walk, and still have been able to return in plenty of time for her appointment with Eye. Dani, off in dreamland, was startled by the sharp rap on her door.

Eye was a slim woman, wore petite glasses, and was a noticeable number of inches shorter than Dani. Dani calculated that she was probably in her middle thirties. Vivacious and assertive, she immediately took charge of their afternoon. As requested in their telephone conversation, Dani was dressed in warm clothing, as the process of hypnosis generally slowed down the heartbeat and she could become chilled.

Eye directed her into the comfortable recliner in the corner of the living room, and moved a chair from the dining-room table over beside the recliner. Eye situated her CD player and pack of CDs on the end table next to the recliner, and inserted the first blank CD. She then walked over to Dani's CD player and caused the room to fill with the soothing compositions of Mother Nature.

Eye sat down on the chair next to Dani. "I want you to close your eyes and try and relax your entire body, and clear all thoughts from your mind except for my instructions." Eye then requested that Dani take a series of deep, deep breaths and to imagine her body relaxing more and more with each deep breath. This was followed by instructions to concentrate on relaxing individual parts of her body, starting with her toes and moving gradually upwards to her neck and head. "After I count to ten, you will be hypnotized when I gently touch your arm. One .... two .... you are becoming more and more relaxed, three .... four .... you are becoming even more relaxed, five .... six .... seven .... you are feeling so relaxed that you are almost asleep, but you will not fall asleep .... eight .... nine .... ten." Eye touched Dani's arm. "You are now in a deep hypnotic trance. You will listen carefully to my instructions, answer my questions, and tell me what you see." Eye gently raised Dani's left arm up above head-level and rested it on her own left hand. As she slowly lowered her hand, Dani's hand descended along with it, back down onto Dani's lap. Eye reached over to the end table and pressed the record button on her CD player. "Are you ready for my instructions?"

"Yes," Dani replied in a barely audible whisper.

"I want you to think back to your early teens, and recall a very happy family occasion in your home. What is the happy occasion?"

"Christmas."
"Who is there with you?"
"My mother and father, and older brother."
"What is your brother's name?"
"Mike."
"Was Mike a good brother?"
"Most of the time."
"Are you good friends, today?"
"Yes."

"I would now like you to go back to another happy occasion, when you were six or seven. What is the happy occasion?"

"My Daddy brought us home a puppy."
"Who picked the name for the puppy?"
"I did."
"What name did you pick?"
"Fluffy."

"I would like you now to go back to another happy event, when you were only one or two years old. What are you doing?"

"I have brown stuff all over my hands and around my mouth."

"Where are you?"
"In my highchair."
"What is the occasion?"
"My first birthday party."

"I want you, now, to go back even further when you were younger and younger, and back even further before you were born. I want you to imagine yourself in a tunnel, a tunnel with lots of space around you and sloping downward like a slide in a playground. You are not afraid. You are going to slide down this tunnel and have a nice ride, okay?"

"Yes."

"Are you afraid?"

"No."

"You are now sliding down this fun-tunnel. It is a little bit dark, but you can see bright sunshine at the bottom of the tunnel. Keep sliding down, and when you reach the bottom you will land on your feet." Eye paused a few seconds. "Are you standing in the sunshine?"

"Yes."

"Look down at the ground under your feet. What do you see?"

"Green grass."

"Look up, now, and slowly turn in a circle, and as you turn, tell me what you see."

"I see green fields, and pasture, forever. Now there is a corral with some animals in it. Cows, pigs, a goat, chickens. Now there is a nice little house, with a covered porch and a railing along the front. There is a man and a young boy playing catch with a ball."

"Do you know them?"

"Yes."

"Who is the man?"

"My husband."

"What is his name?"

"Norman."

"Is the boy your son?"

"Yes."

"What is his name?"

"Normie."

"How old is Normie?"

"Six."

"Do you have any other children?"
"No."
"What is your name?"
"Blanche."
"What is the family name?"
"Ricker."
"Norman, Blanche, and Normie Ricker. Is that correct?"
"Yes."
"What year is it?"
"1892."
"Normie was six in 1892?"
"Yes."
"What country are you living in?"
"The United States."
"Do you live in a town, or out in the country?"
"In the country."
"What is the biggest town near you?"
"Oklahoma City."
"In your current lifetime, do you know the individual who was incarnated as Norman, your husband?"
"No."
"In your current lifetime, do you know the individual who was incarnated as Normie, your son?"
"Yes."
"What is his name in this lifetime?"
"Mike."
"Your brother, Mike, in this lifetime?"
"My brother, Mike."
"I want you to now, once again, picture yourself sliding down the tunnel with the light glowing at the

bottom of it, and land into a different past lifetime than the one as Blanche." Eye reached over and placed a new CD in the recorder. "Are you inside the tunnel?"

"Yes."

"Let me know when you come out of the bottom end of the tunnel."

"I'm out in the sunshine."

"Look at your feet, and tell me what you see."

"Grass."

"Slowly turn in a circle, and as you do, tell me what you see."

"There is lots of green grass and fields. A forest, more green grass, a Castle! There is a girl and a younger boy, playing between the castle and me."

"Who lives in the castle?"

"We do."

"What is your name?"

"Catherine."

"Do you have a husband?"

"Yes."

"What is his name?"

"Douglas. The Earl of Douglas."

"Are the children, that you see playing, the children of Douglas and Catherine?"

"Yes."

"What is the name of the boy?"

"Edward."

"How old is he?"

"Three."

"What is the name of the girl?"

"Margaret."

"How old is Margaret?"

"Five."
"Do you have any other children?"
"No."
"What year is it?"
"1620."
"How long have you lived in the castle?"
"Since I married the Earl."
"What was your maiden name?"
"Foxborough."
"What are, or were, the names of your mother and father?"
"Molly and James."
"Do you have royal blood?"
"Yes."
"What country do you live in?"
"England."
"Where in England do you live?"
"In central England."
"Does the area have a name?"
"The District of Malcolmshire."
"In your current lifetime, do you know the person who was Douglas, your husband then?"
"Yes."
"What is his name, now?"
"Dacque LaRose."
"In your current lifetime, do you know the person who was your daughter, Margaret?"
"No."
"In your current lifetime, do you know the person who was your son, Edward?"
"Yes."
"What is his name, now?"
"Max Winston."

"One more time, I need you to picture yourself back in the tunnel and sliding slowly down towards the light at the bottom."

Eye reached over and changed CDs again. "Let me know when your feet land on the ground."

Eye waited ten or fifteen seconds, but there was no response from Beanpole. "Are you still in the tunnel?"

"No."

"Are you now on the ground?"

"No."

Eye paused for a few moments, searching for the proper expression. "Look down at your feet and tell me what you are standing on, if anything."

"The rung of a ladder."

"Tell me what you see directly in front of you."

"The side of the pyramid."

"Are you telling me that you are standing on the rung of a ladder that is up against a pyramid?"

"Yes."

"What are you doing there?"

"Chipping off the rough edges of the rock to make it line up properly with the stones that it is resting on."

"What year is this?"

"We do not have years."

"Does the area or country where you are have a name?"

"Yes."

"What is that name?"

"Yucatan."

"Are you a man or a woman?"

"A man."

"What is your name?"

"Metamezel."

"Have your ancestors always lived in Yucatan, as far as you are aware of?"

"No."

"Where did they migrate from?"

"Atlantis."

"Can you tell me when they migrated from Atlantis to Yucatan?"

"When they became aware of the immanent expectation of the third huge explosion that would destroy Atlantis."

"Was it your parents who migrated?"

"No."

"What generation of relatives migrated from Atlantis to Yucatan?"

"Great-great-grandparents."

"Do you have a wife or children?"

"No."

"Can you tell me why you have no wife or children?"

"I chose to dedicate my life to God."

"Are your parents still alive?"

"No."

"What was the name of your father?"

"Tantoomezel."

"In your current lifetime, do you know the person who was then your father, Tantoomezel?"

"Yes."

"What is his name, today?"

"Mark Christian."

"In Yucatan, what was the name of your mother?"

"Ta-tanna."

"In your current lifetime, do you know the person who was your mother then, Ta-tanna?"

"Yes."

"What is her name?"

"Nancy Christian."

"Who are Mark and Nancy Christian?"

"My father and mother."

"I am now going to begin to bring you out of your hypnotic trance. You will wake up feeling relaxed and happy, and remember much of the information that you shared with me this afternoon. On the count of ten, you will no longer be hypnotized. One .... two .... three .... you are beginning to be more aware of your surroundings, four .... five .... six .... seven .... you are now almost cognizant of your surroundings, eight .... nine .... ten. Wake up!"

Dani stretched both arms towards the ceiling. Eye turned off the CD recorder. "That went very well," Eye said. "You should be very pleased with the information that we discovered today."

Eyeonthepast handed Dani the three CDs.

Chapter 22
Dancing On Air

Dani was thrilled with the information revealed during her first regression session. She could not sit still for long. She was all ready to go out on her date with Max well before five and paced in circles around her apartment, checking her watch every minute or two. At four forty-five, she headed down to the foyer, hoping that Max would arrive early, and promptly reconvened tracing circles like a figure skater practicing for a competition.

Max stopped in his tracks, inside the door to the foyer, and stared at Dani for a short time. "What in the world is the matter with you?" he demanded.

Dani jumped. She had not seen him enter the building. "I received some interesting information, this afternoon. It's not bad news; it's actually good news. But, I cannot tell you about it right now, and, believe it or not, I can't even tell you why I can't tell you about it right now, if that makes any sense at all?"

"Not much. Are we still going out for the evening?"

"Oh yes! It will be good for me to be distracted from this afternoon's developments."

They had agreed, the day before, that their second real date would be a carbon copy of their first night out on the town, the previous week. On the road to Kathy's Kitchen, Max decided to break the silence. "Are you sure you do not want to tell me what is bugging you?" he asked, guardedly.

"I am truly sorry if it appears that I am taking this out on you, but I swear to you that I am not. Let me try to explain it this way. If you walked into a Japanese language class, how much would you understand?"

"Not one word."

"If I walked into one of your mergers and acquisitions' meetings, how much would I really understand?"

"Probably not much."

"Just like those two examples, what took place this afternoon would effectively be just as impossible for you to make any sense out of. Someday, I assure you, more than you would ever believe, I want to be able to explain all of this to you, and I definitely will work towards doing that, but telling you now, without the proper preliminary groundwork, for sake of a better expression, is pretty much equivalent to abandoning you in a Japanese language class. Please trust me on this. There is nothing wrong. No bad news. Okay?"

"Okay. Not another word."

"That goes for two of us. Let's have a great time tonight."

Chapter 23
Laying The Groundwork

Dani gathered up the Sunday morning breakfast dishes and rinsed them off in the sink. Max stood up from the table and appeared, to Dani, to be preparing to leave for home. "Can you stay another fifteen minutes, please? I would like to discuss something else with you."

Max sat back down at the table and Dani joined him. She took a hand in each of hers, and gave them a reassuring squeeze. "I know you adore me. You not only tell me so, but your actions speak volumes. This conversation will likely turn out to be as confusing as my explanations were last evening in the car, so be forewarned."

"Okay! Shoot."

Dani giggled. "I hope it's not that bad, but here goes. Do you ever think I'm crazy?"

"No. Definitely not! It's obvious that you have secrets that you are not prepared, at least yet, to share with me, and that is fine. I can respect that."

"Good. Do you trust me?"

Max wrinkled his brow. "Yeees," he said, dragging it out.

"That didn't sound very reassuring!"

"Sorry. Yes, I definitely trust you, but I have no idea where you are going with this."

"Bear with me a little longer. I'll be back in a minute."

Dani walked over to her computer desk and returned with a book. "I need you to read this."

Max recognized it as the one he momentarily looked at on the night of their first date. "I really don't have time to read novels."

"It's not a novel, it's a biography."

"Oh. Of who?"

"Some long-deceased gentleman you probably never heard of, but will never forget after you read the book. You told me you trusted me. Please read this book, a little at a time when you are able to steal a few minutes. After you are finished, I will be ready to share my secrets with you because you will be better prepared to understand them. Please? For me?"

Max picked up the book and stared at it. There Is a River, by Thomas Sugrue. Interesting name for a biography, he thought to himself. "Okay, I will do it. I promise. Do I have a deadline?"

"No. Take all of the time you need. Let me know when you are finished."

Chapter 24
Reliving A Past Lifetime

Monday morning, Dani called Dacque after eight and arranged to meet him at his apartment complex to accompany him on his usual walk, and to follow it up with a past-lives discussion.

Their walk completed, Dacque invited Dani up to his apartment for a cold drink. Dani had told Dacque about her past-lives regression session with Eye, but walking around the streets of Anywhere was no place to discuss reincarnation and past lives.

Lounging in Dacque's living room, Dani reintroduced the topic. "In your regression sessions with Eye, did the name of Douglas, the Earl of Douglas ever come up?"

Dacque's face lit up instantly, like a light bulb reacting to the flick of a switch. "Yes! Yes! Yes! Did I show up in your past lives?" he almost screamed.

"Yes. Do you have your notes from that session?"

"Yes, I'll go get them. I think I remember the information revealed, but at my age I can get things mixed up if I haven't looked at them recently." Dacque retrieved the notebook that contained the highlights from his past-life regressions and returned to the living room.

"Can I use your CD player?" Dani asked, removing a CD from her purse.

"Certainly. I can't wait to hear this."

Dani pushed the start button and sat back down. They listened in silence to Eye eliciting the information from Dani on her incarnation as

Catherine, wife of the Earl of Douglas. Dani glanced over at Dacque after the CD player clicked off, and noticed the tears trickling down his cheeks. She immediately burst into tears herself, jumped up off the couch and ran into Dacque's outstretched arms.

"I have found you! I have found you! This is marvelous news! Marvelous! Marvelous! Marvelous!" Dacque shouted through his tears.

"I know! I know it is," Dani whispered into his ear as she clung tightly to his quivering body.

"I told you there was a plan! I told you!"

"You certainly did," Dani assured him. "All my doubts have disintegrated. And, I could not believe how Max was there, also. I was shocked."

They sat down on the sofa, side by side and compared notes. Dacque's reading had not revealed the current incarnation for Catherine or Edward, their son, because Dacque had not known Dani and Max at the time of his session, three years earlier.

Dani could not identify their daughter Margaret, but it turned out, she was the only one that Dacque was able to identify. She was reincarnated as Isabel, his daughter.

"Does Max know anything about this?" Dacque asked.

"Not a thing. Only yesterday, I passed on to him your copy of There Is a River, and had a tough time arm-twisting him into promising to read it. He said he would, and I believe him. He has always been true to his word with me."

"Do you think he would ever have a regression session?" Dacque asked.

"That's a tough one," Dani responded. "He is so practical that it will certainly be an uphill battle. We will just have to be patient and see how he comes around."

Chapter 25
Dreaming Past Lives

Dani had mixed emotions before her Friday morning walk with Dacque. She was excited to be starting her new job at Williams, Bradford and Williams on Monday, but sad that it might be their last walk together for the foreseeable future. Monday to Friday, she would be at work at the usual time Dacque ventured forth on his morning walks, and Max habitually stayed overnight with her on Fridays and Saturdays. She was not prepared to chase him out the door until he was good and ready to depart for his weekend overtime at the office, which had never once been anywhere near nine o'clock. Under those circumstances, Dani decided that Friday was the logical time to bring up a new development in her past-lives, educational dossier. For their last, foreseeable walk together, Dani had requested that they meet on their bench in MacDunnah Park and, as much as possible, retrace their steps from the first day they had been brought together by unexpected circumstances or Heavenly Manipulation.

The always punctual Dani was waiting for Dacque on their special bench well before his arrival. He settled in beside her and they exchanged cordial pleasantries, but Dani quickly detoured the conversation to a topic that had been weighing heavily on her mind for a few days. "Dacque, do you ever have dreams about your past lives?"

Dacque shot her a startled look, and broke into a smile. "Yes, sometimes. I assume that you have had some?"

"Yes, but just on our lifetime together in England."

"Don't say another word, please. This presents us with a wonderful and rare opportunity to do some unique research."

"It does?"

"Yes. Let me explain. I too have been having dreams, this week, about our life together in England. I suspect that over the years I may have had dreams about all of my past lives, but I did not always write them down. I know better now. I had not experienced dreams about my life as the Earl of Douglas, in England, for some time, but since we recently discovered our connection in that lifetime, I have been having dreams every night about the Earl of Douglas."

"Me too," Dani added, excitedly.

"We must not reveal the details of these dreams to each other, right now. I have a way of attempting to determine whether we are having the same dream, without revealing too much, or whether we are just both dreaming of the same time period because we were both thrilled to discover our past lives together."

"I understand," Dani assured him, and stood up. "Are we ready to walk?"

"Definitely."

As the noon hour approached, Dacque insisted that he would treat her to lunch, as he had that first day. Dani protested but knew full well that it was a lost cause.

After the conclusion of lunch, Dacque suggested, if she had the time, that they walk back to his apartment, and commence their study of their dreams of Catherine and Douglas in England.

Dacque settled into an easy chair, after retrieving a notepad and pencil from his desk. "Try to keep your descriptions or answers to a word or two, please," he said to Dani. "You will soon get the hang of it, once we get rolling. Okay?"

"Okay."

"My dream on Monday night involved a horse race," Dacque advised Dani. "Did you have a dream with a horse race?"

"No."

"In a word or two, what was your Monday-night dream about, if you had one that night?"

"Margaret's wedding."

"I did not dream about that," Dacque stated. "My Tuesday-night dream involved some kind of a battle. I was wounded. Does that ring a bell?"

"Not at all."

"Describe, briefly, your Tuesday night dream."

"Margaret had a baby."

"We are not doing very well, here. I did not have that one, either," Dacque advised. "My Wednesday night dream involved a feast, but I would be hard-pressed to describe it as a wedding feast. Sound familiar?"

"Not really."

"What was your third dream about?"

"It was Edward's wedding," Dani said.

"Not a match, once again. Last night's dream, apparently involved my teaching Edward how to shoot a bow-and-arrow."

"My dream last night was of the death of my father. We are obviously not having similar dreams. What does this all mean?" Dani asked.

"If we were having simultaneous dreams, this would likely imply a psychic connection. One of us might begin the dream, and the other would somehow psychically tune-in to that dream. This is rare. Because we are not having identical dreams, we are most likely just having these dreams because we are excited to have found our past-life connection, and we have called-up past memories from our subconscious minds, involving events memorable to us."

"I guess that makes sense," Dani added.

"Please continue to write down all that you can remember about any past-life dreams, and periodically we will try to find time to quiz each other about them. Just because we are not currently having simultaneous dreams, does not mean that we never could."

"I recorded the first four, and I will continue to do so."

"Good. There is one other psychic activity, that is also very rare, but I want to mention it just in case you experience it. There are two people, in our Reincarnation Enlightenment Group, who seem to be able to recall when they are together and totally awake, events that they shared in past lives."

"Wow! That would be awesome," Dani commented.

"It certainly would."

Dani stood up, and stretched. "I guess I better start my walk back home. I have lots of things to contemplate on the journey."

Chapter 26
Dacque's Story

Dani's first week at Williams, Bradford and Williams was uneventful, pleasant but uneventful. When Max asked about plans for their Saturday evening on-the-town, Dani advised him that she would like to cook Saturday's dinner and invite Dacque over to join them.

Dani shooed Max and Dacque into the living room after dinner, and began to clean up the kitchen.

Dacque wasted little time getting to the heart of his interests. "Dani tells me that you recently completed reading Thomas Sugrue's, There Is a River. What did you think of it?"

Max was somewhat shocked that Dani mentioned this fact to Dacque, but his quick-thinking abilities camouflaged his surprise. "Well, if it is a true account, then Edgar Cayce was a most unusual gentleman. It would have been virtually impossible to fake thousands of medical readings, and he sure had some interesting surprises for the doctors. I'm not as convinced about the reincarnation material, but it would be nigh impossible for him to manufacture all of those past lives that he uncovered, so it is difficult to condemn him as a forger. I gather you are familiar with the gentleman, or the book. What do you think?"

"For a number of years now, I have been convinced that Edgar Cayce was a true miracle man. The medical readings convinced me, but it is the reincarnation readings that have commanded my attention. I have been researching survival of the soul and reincarnation for over ten years now. Would you care to hear how that all got started?"

"Sure," Max replied. "Why not?"

Dani had been eavesdropping on their conversation from the kitchen area. She quickly dried her hands and settled down on the sofa beside Max.

"It was about twelve years ago when the doctors discovered that my wife had colon cancer. Unfortunately, it was too far advanced, and she passed away six months later. Our children and grandchildren literally live all over the world. After the funeral, their busy lives called them back to their various locations, and I was alone, facing a new existence that I had not experienced for four decades. We lived in a fairly large old house in Canton, Ohio, for most of our married life, and after my wife was gone, I just worked at surviving one day at a time. No real plans, other than to survive for another day.

"My wife's birthday was about a month after her passing, and as the date drew near, my dread multiplied enormously. I always tried to celebrate her birthday in a unique way, and there I was, bewildered and befuddled as to what I should do, if anything, for her birthday. I decided to buy a dozen roses, and placed them in her favorite vase on the kitchen counter. Next to the vase, I placed my favorite picture of her.

"On our refrigerator, there was a pretty magnet that I purchased for her decades earlier. We both loved the saying: You Light up My Life! It lived on the top, right-hand corner of the freezer door so long; it effectively became part of the door. At bedtime, for some reason, I got the notion that I should remove the magnet and place it in front of the flowers and the picture, and I am pretty sure I did.

"In the morning, I almost had a heart attack when I noticed that the magnet was back in its home on the top, right-hand corner of the freezer door. I was positive that I moved that magnet to the counter, but wondered, in my grief, if I had only planned to do it, then neglected to do so. That night, I diligently removed the magnet and placed it on the counter with the flowers and the picture. The next morning the magnet was back home on the refrigerator. For one solid week, I placed that magnet on the counter each night, and every morning it was back on the top right corner of the freezer door. At that point I was unequivocally convinced that my wife wanted the magnet to remain in its home on the fridge. The roses were on their last legs, so I threw them out and returned the picture to our bedroom night table.

"Wow," Dani commented. "That is amazing!"

"The story has only just begun," Dacque advised his stunned listeners.

"Oh! We're all ears," Dani replied.

"My wife did not snore, much, only when she was lying in one certain position, on her back, and even then, not real loud. Not too long after the magnet incidents, I was awake in the middle of the night, for whatever reason, and I heard her unique snore from the other side of the bed. There was no one else in the house, just me. I propped myself up on one elbow and looked at the other side of the bed. I could not see anyone, but the snoring continued. I reached my right hand over to touch her, but there was no one there. When I did, the snoring stopped. This occurred at least three different nights. I could hear her as plain as day, but I could not touch her. Then, one evening I was sitting on the sofa reading a book, and I happened to glance over at the easy chair, and my breath stopped. My wife was sitting in her favorite chair, looking unbelievably beautiful, as if she were thirty again. She smiled at me and said: 'You must stop grieving and get on with your life. I am fine. There is no more pain.' Then, poof, she disappeared. After that evening there were no further incidents.

"From that point on, I had no doubts that our spirits, or souls, or whatever, lived on after our bodies died. I started to seriously research survival of souls, and one of the first things I did was to reread Thomas Sugrue's There Is a River." Dacque stopped his narrative, and awaited a reaction.

"What do you think about that, Max?" Dani asked.

Max hesitated and carefully chose his words. "It truly is an amazing story, and it is easy to see why you believe in survival of the soul. Did you learn anything else in your research?"

"Yes," Dacque replied. "Belief in survival of the soul naturally led to reincarnation of souls. After I moved from Canton to Anywhere, I discovered a group of individuals who believed in reincarnation. One of the founding members of the group is a certified regression therapist, and in non-working hours, she provides free hypnotic regression sessions for members of this group. Over a period of a year or so, I had three sessions with her, and discovered about a dozen different past lives, some back further than you would ever imagine. In some of those incarnations, I was able to identify individuals reincarnated with me in this lifetime."

"Just like Edgar Cayce did?" Max commented.

"The same idea," Dacque replied. He stared at Dani, hoping that she was prepared to jump into the fray.

She was. "Max, do you remember, two weeks ago tonight, when I was acting very strange and wearing circles into carpets? I would not tell you why?"

"Yes, I remember."

"Only a few hours before our date, I had my first past-life regression session, with this lady Dacque spoke of, and discovered three of my past lifetimes. That is why I was so excited, and had to be so secretive, because if I told you then, you definitely would have thought I was crazy. But, there is still more. In one of my three past lifetimes, I was incarnated with Dacque, and ..." Dani hesitated, "and you were incarnated then, with us."

Max sighed. "Tell me you are making up all of this?"

"It's true, Max. I swear. You know that I would never lie to you, and you cannot deny that. Dacque had already discovered that same incarnation years ago, way before he ever met us, so he was unable to identify us at that time."

Max sighed, again. "Yes, I know you would never lie to me. Tell me about our past life together."

Dani looked across at Dacque.

"We really should not do that, yet," Dacque responded.

"Explain, please," Max replied.

"The proper next step, here, is for you to have a regression session with this lady, or any reputable hypnotist, and see what you uncover about your past lives. That way, you will be more convinced of the truth of this process, than if we just tell you."

"I am a very well-respected lawyer in this city. I can't be taking hypnotic journeys with a regression therapist and have it spread all over the city."

"We understand, Max. Many of us feel exactly the same way," Dacque advised. "The members of this reincarnation group, that I talked about, all use an alias and a specific email address for their group communications. Hardly anyone knows who the others are, with a few exceptions, like Dani and I, as I was the one who recommended that the group accept her as a member. Either of us can do the same for you."

"I had my hypnotic session here in my apartment," Dani added, "but the hypnotist did not know my name, nor do I know hers. If you would like, you could also have your session here in my apartment, and there is no way she could identify you, even if she wanted to."

"I understand," Max said pensively. "Let me think about this for a while."

"Take all of the time you need," Dani replied. "When you are ready, we can make the process work, totally incognito."

Chapter 27
Surprise, Surprise

Exactly ten days had zipped by since Dacque had sat contentedly in Dani's living room and recounted, to Dani and Max, the apparent activity of the departed spirit of his wife, and his resulting belief in, and investigation of, reincarnation. Max had spent at least a few hours with Dani on every one of those days, and never once mentioned Dacque's story or their encouragement that he request a past-life regression session for himself.

"Here is my special, new email address," he said to Dani on Tuesday evening, right out of the blue. "My code name is Tackle, from my football days. If you or Dacque get me registered with the group, I am willing to try a regression session this weekend, if it can be worked out."

"That is wonderful news!" Dani declared, and gave him a warm hug and a kiss. "I will get right on it."

"I would like to have the session here in your apartment, if that is still alright with you?" Max added, after their embrace. "I definitely need to take the utmost precaution to conceal my identity, and to use my own house would not be wise."

"I understand completely. I was the one who suggested my apartment, originally, I believe?"

"I remember. That option was definitely instrumental in making the decision to do this. Now, while we are on the topic of my house, I would like you to come to my house for a nice dinner, tomorrow night."

Dani was surprised. She had never before been invited to Max's abode. Now and then she had mused about why this never occurred, but it had not really bothered her that much. She knew that Max lived in a large, historical mansion on Lake-Of-Many-Bays, a fifteen or twenty minute drive north of Anywhere, but he had always been at-home in her meager surroundings. He mentioned, more than once, that he had spent most of his life in similar establishments. "You told me many times that you didn't cook. What are you serving, peanut butter and jam sandwiches?"

Max roared. "That's an idea. Glad you thought of it," he teased. "Actually, my cook will take care of everything."

"Your cook? You never mentioned a cook, before. When are you ever home to need a cook?"

"I have a secret. Of course I don't need a cook, but, unfortunately, my job requires me to entertain rich clients, most of who would not settle for peanut butter and jam sandwiches. I have a Personal Management Agency that looks after all of my pampering needs. I tell them when and what I require and they provide the miracles. What would you like served for dinner?"

"You can't be serious?"

"Perfectly serious! What is your favorite dish?"

Dani mulled over her options for a few moments. "You know that I am not much for stuffy settings. Can I assume this will be a casual evening?"

"Done, but we need to fill your plate."

"You know, I have not had a nice roast of pork in years. How about roast pork and apple sauce?"

"And vegetables, and dessert?"

"Surprise me. Nothing fancy, remember?"

"While we are into surprises, my mother has invited me, and my new girlfriend, over for dinner on Saturday evening. I gather she wants to check you out herself, probably to verify my bragging about your beauty and personality. By the way, it will not be a fancy dinner there, either. More Momma's home cooking. Right up our line."

"That sounds wonderful, Max. I hope you did not build me up too much. I would hate to see her disappointed."

"I only told her the truth. She will love you."

Chapter 28
Max's Mansion

Max picked up Dani at her apartment, in his spotless, white Cadillac, and drove her to his house on Lake-Of-Many-Bays. Dani had changed into casual attire, but Max was still in his expensive suit, as he had come directly from his law office.

Max turned his Cadillac into a gated driveway, and slowly approached the house, partially obscured from the front of the property by numerous trees. As the vehicle exited from this mini-forest, Dani got her first, clear view of his historic mansion. It immediately reminded her of the southern mansions often depicted in the movies. After parking his vehicle directly in front of the door, Max hustled around to open the passenger door for Dani.

Dani stood, effectively paralyzed, inside the entranceway. She had never experienced anything like this. The double-wide, red carpeted staircase in front of her led up to a horse-shoe-shaped balcony that over-looked the two-story entranceway on all sides except the front. It was decorated with, she assumed, expensive portraits from the past, and numerous statues and other antiques. The tiled entranceway housed matching sitting areas on the left and on the right.

A woman in a maid's uniform appeared from behind the staircase. "Good evening Mr. Winston, Miss."

"Good evening, Rosie. I would like you to meet Miss Christian," Max responded.

"I am pleased to meet you, Miss Christian," Rosie said, extending her hand to Dani. "Dinner will be ready shortly."

"Thank you, Rosie. We will be around," Max advised.

Rosie disappeared once again behind the massive staircase.

Dani looked up at Max. "I would never have imagined that you lived in a place like this. I'm not sure exactly what I expected, but this certainly exceeds anything I could have anticipated."

"It's all part of the show," Max declared. "I really had no intention of living in a mansion like this. It all happened by accident, actually. The owner of this place was a good friend of one of the partners of the law firm, Mr. Kluzewski. The gentleman passed away after a short illness, and his widow decided that she would move up north and live with a daughter. The law firm's partners had been on my back for quite some time, suggesting that I should have a nice home in which I could entertain clients, so, when this house suddenly became available, Mr. Kluzewski advised me to purchase it.

"It was never offered on the open market. I purchased it just like you see it, including the furniture and antiques. I really did not need this place, or so I thought, but I realized that it would be a good investment even if I decided not to stay here forever. I primarily use three rooms in the entire place - my bedroom, the library, and the kitchen, where I eat at a smaller table. There are rooms up there," Max said, waving his arm towards the closed doors around the horse-shoe-shaped balcony, "that I have not been in, in months. When I have guests, some of the extra bedrooms do get used, as, of course, does the dining room where we shall dine this evening.

"I am going to run upstairs and change into something more casual, before dinner. Have a seat, or browse around wherever you like. Nothing is out of bounds."

Max hustled up the tall staircase, and Dani decided to slowly circle the entranceway, which, she estimated, occupied about one-quarter of the entire mansion. All of the doors under the balcony were closed and she decided against peeking behind any of them. Arriving back at the staircase, Dani slowly climbed the soft-carpeted steps to the balcony. Max had entered a doorway at the top of the stairs, so Dani decided she would mosey along the balcony to the left, and check out the artwork and antiques, which she knew very little about anyway.

When she reached the end of the balcony, she checked to see if Max had reappeared, and not seeing him, gambled on peeking into the room in front of her. Slowly, she opened the door and stepped inside a large bedroom. It housed a good-sized canopy bed, and, to her anyway, a room full of antique furniture. She had never toured a southern mansion, but she envisioned that their bedrooms would probably look just like the one in front of her. The idle thought, which tumbled across her mind, was stale. This was a place you saw in magazines, not a place that real people lived in. Dani heard a door close behind her, and turned to see Max walking her way, a smile on his face.

"I see you had a chance to look around. What do you think?"

Dani chose her words carefully. "It reminds me of something from the movies, or a magazine. It is very striking."

"But not someplace the average person would want to live in?" Max added.

"I didn't say that!" Dani protested.

"I know, I know," Max said, placing his hand gently on her shoulder. "This is really not me, either. I feel more comfortable lounging around your apartment than I do in my own house, if that makes any sense at all?"

"It does. You act the part only because you are expected to."

"Mr. Winston," a voice called from the first floor. "Dinner is ready."

"We are on our way, Rosie."

Chapter 29
Unimaginable Revelation

Max and Dani fidgeted nervously as they sat on the sofa in Dani's living room and watched the hands on the clock turtle along. Eyeonthepast had offered to hold Max's first, past-life regression session on Saturday afternoon at one, and Max had eagerly accepted her offer. Dani and Max jumped at the sound of the loud rap on the apartment door.

"Good afternoon Eye. You probably remember me? I'm Beanpole," Dani said, as she opened the door. "Please come in. This is my good friend, Tackle," she added as Max extended his hand to their visitor.

"I am pleased to meet you, Tackle, and thank you for joining the Reincarnation Enlightenment Group. Are you excited about your first regression session?"

"Yes," Max replied. "A little nervous but excited."

"Well, I recommend that we get right to it then, so you have no more time to be nervous. Beanpole, did you plan on remaining in the apartment during the session?"

"No. I understood that was frowned upon, so I made other plans. Tackle can call me when the session is over."

"Great. That's the way I prefer it," Eye confirmed.

Dani picked up her purse and left the apartment. Eye wasted little time, and began her standard procedures for beginning a regression session. Once Max made himself comfortable in Dani's recliner,

Eye efficiently regressed him into a deep hypnotic state.

"I would like you to imagine that you are sliding down a tunnel, a roomy tunnel with a gradual downward slope. At the end of the tunnel you can see a light. The light gets brighter and brighter as you slide closer to it. When you reach the end of the tunnel, you will land on your feet in a previous lifetime. Tell me when you are standing on the ground."

Tackle was silent for a few seconds. "I am on the ground."

"Please turn in a circle, and tell me what you see."

"There is a large crowd of people. Lots of women and children. Many of them are crying and hugging men in white uniforms. There is an enormous ship behind us."

"Are you wearing a white uniform, too?"

"Yes."

"Can you tell me your name?"

"Jed, Jed Ricker."

The name jogged Eye's memory. She could remember hearing it within the past few weeks. "Can you tell me what year it is?"

"1944."

"Are you sailing off on the ship, shortly?"

"Yes."

"Is your family there to see you off?"

"Yes."

"Is your wife there?"

"Yes."

"What is her name?"

"Mavis Ricker."

"If your children are there also, please tell me their names and ages."

"Doris is there. She is four."

"Do you have any other children?"

"No."

"Are your parents there also?"

"No."

"Do they live far away?"

"They have both passed away."

"What were the names of your mother and father?"

"Alice and Norman Ricker."

"Are any of the close relatives of Jed Ricker known to you in your current lifetime? If so, please identify them in both lifetimes."

"Doris is my mother, and Mavis Ricker was my grandmother."

"Has your grandmother passed away?"

"Yes."

Eye removed the CD from the recorder to her right, and replaced it with a blank. "I would like you to once again imagine that you are sliding down the same tunnel as before, but when you reach the end, you will land in a different, previous lifetime. Will you let me know when you exit from the tunnel?"

"Yes." Tackle was silent for a few seconds, as he completed his ride. "I am out of the tunnel."

"Look around and tell me what you see."

"There is a big party, a wedding party."

"Whose wedding is it?"

"Mine."

"What is your name?"

"Edward of Douglas."

"What are the names of your mother and father?"
"Catherine and Douglas."
"What is the year, when you are being married?"
"1641."
"What is the name of your new wife?"
"Elizabeth."
"If you have any brothers or sisters, will you please tell me their names and ages?"
"Margaret is twenty-six, and Henry is ten."
"What country do you live in?"
"England."
"Does your area, region or town have a name and if so what is it called?"
"The District of Malcolmshire."
"Are any of the close relatives of Edward, known to you in your current lifetime? If so, please identify them in both lifetimes."
"My mother, Catherine, is Dani Christian, and my father, Douglas, is Dacque LaRose."

Eye reached over once again and replaced the CD with a blank one. "You will now take one more ride down the tunnel and land this time in an incarnation different from the previous two that you have told me about today. Please let me know when you are out of the tunnel."

"I am out of the tunnel."
"Please tell me what you see."
"We are riding on horses, in formation."
"What is your name?"
"Jonathan Mac Grab."
"How old are you, Jonathan?"
"Twenty-seven."
"What year is it?"

"889."
"Are you a soldier?"
"Yes."
"Who is your leader?"
"King Domnall."
"What is the name of King Domnall's kingdom?"
"The Nation of the Picts."
"Do you have a wife or children?"
"No."
"Are your parents alive?"
"Yes."
"Please tell me their names."
"Enoch and Bethane Mac Grab."
"Do you have any brothers and sisters?"
"I had a sister, but she became ill, and died."
"What was her name?"
"Bethany."
"Are any of your close relatives as Jonathan Mac Grab known to you in your current lifetime?"
"Enoch Mac Grab is my father."

Eye looked at her watch. She had a second appointment to attend to, and it was becoming apparent that Tackle was beginning to get tired. "I am now going to bring you gradually out of your hypnotic trance. You will wake up feeling refreshed, and remember most of the events and names that you have recounted to me this afternoon. Can you do that?"

"Yes."

"On the count of ten, you will no longer be hypnotized. One ...... two ...... three, you are beginning to feel more alert, four ...... five ...... six ......

seven, you are almost fully conscious, eight ...... nine ...... ten. Wake up."

Max stretched his arms in the air, rocked his shoulders back and forth, and opened his eyes.

"We had an excellent session, Tackle. You should be very pleased." Eye handed him the three CDs. "Here is your record of the three incarnations that you shared with me today. They contain some important history."

"Thank you, and thank you for holding this session for me. Can I pay you something for this?"

"No, it is gratis. If you come to a group meeting, someday, you can, if you like, drop some cash into the group donation box. Just cash, no identification, okay?"

"Yes, and thank you again."

Chapter 30
Family Connections

As soon as Eye departed from Dani's apartment, Max called Dani.

"Hi Max. How did it go?"

"Amazing! I found our incarnation together back in England, but the information on my most recent past life blew me away. I am the reincarnation of my grandfather, Jed Ricker, who was in the US Navy and was lost at sea in 1945 near Japan."

"Max! Say his name again, slowly."

"Jed Rick...er. Why?"

"I had an incarnation in the 19th century as Blanche Ricker. Does that name ring a bell?"

"No, but the Ricker name has been in the family for generations. Guess who the family genealogist is?"

"I don't know."

"None other than the lady who is cooking dinner for us this evening. My mother has a box full of charts and old photos dating back a couple of hundred years, and sometimes longer. She loves to dig the box out and show visitors her treasured information. I must admit, I never had much interest in the family genealogy. I guess that just changed. If Blanche Ricker is related to our Rickers, my mother should be able to tell you."

"Great! I can't wait! I'm on my way home. Bye."

"Bye."

Chapter 31
Opening The Soul Mind

After the delicious, pot-roast dinner had added inches to waistlines, Dani insisted on helping Max's mother with the clean-up, while Max and his father settled into comfortable chairs in the living room, to catch up. Although they only lived thirty minutes apart, Max's fifty-hour-plus work-weeks, and the recent introduction of Dani into his life, had cut into his visits with his parents.

"How are you boys making out?" Max's mother asked as she and Dani joined the men in the living room.

"Just catching up on the news," responded Max's dad, Fred.

"Mom," Max said after a brief pause in the conversation, "are you interested in getting out your box of genealogy information? It turns out that Dani had a Ricker ancestor, and we were curious whether there was a connection to our family, somewhere in there."

Doris' eyes lit up. "You know it doesn't take much encouragement for me to get out the infamous box."

"I know," Max chuckled, as his mother deftly engineered a quick U-turn.

In less than two minutes, almost a new record, Doris Winston returned with the infamous box. She set it on the dining room table and removed the lid. "Okay, Dani, what information do you have?"

"Mom," Max interrupted, hesitantly, "there is one other piece of information that we need to give you. Dani and I have recently become believers in survival of the soul after death, and reincarnation. Dani's Ricker ancestor is from her previous lifetime, not this one."

Doris' mouth dropped, and she stared at her son for what felt like an eternity to the others in the room. "Oh. Okay. I understand. Well, maybe I don't really understand. What, I guess, I'm trying to say is that I understand what you said, but I'm not sure I understand how that would work."

"Some of us believe that when a human body dies," Dani explained, "that the spirit and soul of the person does not die, but lives on, in Heaven, if you prefer the term, or in another dimension where most humans cannot see them. Then, many years, or even centuries later, a soul usually has another incarnation by entering the body of a new-born baby. Often this new-born baby has a connection in some way, and there are numerous possible past-connections I should add, to a past life of its new soul. It is really difficult to try to comprehend all of this from a few words, but it is possible for a trained regression therapist, or hypnotist, to encourage a hypnotized subject to go back in time, and peek into previous lifetimes. A few weeks ago, I had one of these regression sessions, and uncovered three of my previous lifetimes. In one of them I was named Ricker."

Max's mother remained silent for a few more seconds. "The whole idea sounds rather mind boggling, but let's just ignore that aspect, for the present, anyway. What information do you have on the Rickers?"

"All that I have is a Norman married a Blanche. They had a young son they called Normie, and lived in the country near Oklahoma City."

Doris rustled through her box of treasures and removed some papers. She flipped through a few until she located the one she was apparently looking for, and glanced at it for a few seconds. A smile broke out on her lips as she tossed the papers on the table and frantically rooted through the box again.

Removing a photo in a cardboard frame, she stood up and walked towards Dani. Handing the picture to Dani, she said, "That is a photo of Blanche Ricker, my great-grandmother."

Dani looked at the photo for a moment, clutched it to her chest then broke into tears. "That's me. That's me," she blubbered through her tears. The latch on the door from her soul mind buckled under the pressure and long-entombed past memories flowed out like molten lava down the sides of an erupting volcano. She looked at Doris. "You are my little Dorie, my sweet little Dorie. You were my reason for living the last few years of my life. I could not wait for you to come home from school and spend time with me. I read stories to you, then when you were in grade one and learned to read, you would hop up beside me on my bed and read to me from your school reader, all about the escapades of Dick and Jane. You loved the story of Little Red Riding Hood, and wanted me to read it to you almost every day. I can see it all as if it occurred just yesterday."

Doris stepped into Dani's arms and they sobbed on each other's shoulders. "I never, in a million lifetimes, could have imagined this," Doris blubbered.

Chapter 32
Reminiscing

After Dani and Doris discovered their past connection as Blanche and Dorie, they spent the remainder of the evening sharing stories and information. Max and Fred were not the least bit bored listening to the excited ladies, as the vast majority of their discussion about their decade together over sixty years before, was new news to both of the men. Max's heart warmed as the obvious bond forming, between his mother and his new love, multiplied before his eyes.

After an extended period of sharing past memories, Doris picked up the family genealogy chart and explained the relevant portions to Dani. "Norman Ricker and Blanche Woodward were born and raised in central Georgia. A year or so after their marriage, they decided to seek their fortune in the west, converted their meager assets into cash, and took off on the train. Apparently for no known reason, they liked the area around Oklahoma City. They decided to remain there for a while, and never left. Norman worked for a farmer, or rancher, before they bought some land of their own. They had Norman Jr. or Normie as you call him, and a number of years later, a girl named Melissa. Melissa married a fellow from California and they lived out there. I do not think I ever met her or her family.

"Norman Jr. followed his father into farming, married a local girl called Alice Jamieson, and they stayed on the farm with you, or Blanche, and his father. Your Norman passed away in 1930 at sixty-eight. Alice only had one child, a son named Jedediah, my father. He was commonly called Jed. He was born in 1916, and died near Japan in 1945, when his ship was torpedoed. He had no interest in farming, and joined the US Navy when he was twenty."

At the mention of Jed, Dani glanced over at Max with a knowing smile.

Max returned the smile, but said nothing. His story could wait. There was no way he was going to interrupt his mother's dissertation to Dani on their family connections.

"Both Norm Jr. and Alice died way too young. He went in 1941 at age fifty-five, and Alice joined him in 1942, at fifty-one. You, Blanche, still owned the farm outside of Oklahoma City, but you were the last Ricker left in the area. My mother told me that my father adored you, Blanche. He had lived in the family house, your house, all of his life until he left home and joined the navy. He met my mother, Mavis Marshall, when he was stationed at Newport, Rhode Island, where my mother grew up. My mother was married at nineteen, and had me at twenty.

"After you, or Blanche, sold the farm in Oklahoma, you came north to be near my father. You had way more money than my parents, so you bought a house in Newport and invited our family to move in with you. I think I may have been two. My father was away at sea a lot, so most of the time it was apparently only my mother and I living with you. After we entered the war, Dad was home very little. In the fall of 1944, my mother and I saw him off at the docks in Newport. I think I was four. I still remember that day. I was crying and begging him not to leave. I sometimes wonder if I had a premonition, but maybe I was simply old enough to understand that I did not want my father to leave again. He never came back.

"I don't know what would have happened to us if we were not living in your house. My mother worked when she could. There were periods I saw more of you than I did of her. I called you Grandma Blanche, because my mother did, even though you were my great-grandmother. You were over eighty then, and were becoming frail and sickly. You died in 1950, at the age of eighty-six. You willed the house to my mother and she lived there for another fifty years until she passed away in 2000."

Chapter 33
Max's Surprise

The past-life discussions between Doris and Dani on Saturday evening continued until almost eleven, and probably could have lasted for hours longer. They were brought to a conclusion after Doris announced that she was becoming rather tired, and should be thinking about going to bed. In the midst of the numerous thank you's, hugs and goodbyes, Max mentioned that if his parents were free on Sunday afternoon, that he and Dani would like to return and share some other surprises with them. They agreed upon a one-thirty arrival.

Fred and Doris warmly greeted Max and Dani. Max carried Dani's CD player under his arm, as he could not recall whether his parents actually had one of their own. It was a wise move, as his parents were still operating from a cassette-tape player.

After the four of them were seated comfortably in the living room, Max plugged in the CD player and inserted a CD. "I had my first past-life regression session just yesterday afternoon. It was interesting, to say the least. I received information on three of my past lifetimes, over a period of an hour or so, but one in particular is going to be of great interest to you," Max said, looking at his mother. "Instead of telling you about it, I think it is best for you to listen to it, just as I described it under hypnosis. It will also give you an idea of what takes place during a regression session. Mom, you might want to grab a box of tissues."

"Oh! Okay."

After Doris returned and settled down on the sofa beside Fred, Max started the CD on his incarnation as Jed Ricker. Max was on-the-money. Doris cried throughout most of the CD.

Dani also joined her at times.

"Can you play that again, Max, please?" Doris asked. "I know I missed some of it while I was blubbering. I'll try not to cry the second time around."

Doris was true to her word, and did not cry. "I wish I could tell you more about my father, but the main memory I seem to have of him was that day on the docks, saying goodbye."

"That's okay, Mom," Max said. "I understand. You were very young, then."

"You said that you discovered three past incarnations?" Doris said to Max. "Are we going to listen to all three?"

"I did not bring the other CDs, Mom. You were apparently not with me in the other two incarnations."

"We still could have listened to them, couldn't we?"

"That's actually not recommended," Dani chirped in.

"Why not?"

"Is there a chance that you might like to investigate some of your past incarnations?" Dani asked.

"I don't know. Maybe. Does that matter?"

"I have been advised that it could," Dani replied. "Apparently it is best if we don't consciously know, ahead of time, about the past lives of our relatives and friends, just in case that knowledge might influence which past lives show up in a regression session. We really should not have shared Max's incarnation as Jed with you, but it was unconscionable to keep the information a secret from you.

"Supposedly, the past lives that we uncover in our earlier sessions are those incarnations which are most significant to our current lifetime. Just because two people had an incarnation together in the past, does not automatically make that incarnation significant to this lifetime, if that makes any sense?"

"Not much, if you want the truth."

Dani laughed. "Anyway, we were told not to share information on past incarnations with anyone, at least until both parties have determined that they have had an incarnation together. If you think either of you would be interested in learning about some of your past lives, let us know, and we can work on setting up a session for you."

"I'll mull it over for a while," Doris said. "What do you think, Fred?"

"I'll give it some thought."

Chapter 34
Catching Up

Monday, on her lunch break, Dani called Dacque.
"Hello."
"Hello. This is your favorite Chinese-food restaurant calling you with our daily specials."
"Oh," Dacque replied, recognizing Dani's voice. "I thought you went out of business."
"Smarty! It hasn't been that long. Are you free at dinner time?"
"You tell me."
"I will call you when I get out of work. I have not been working nearly as much overtime at this new firm, as I was with Max, so it will likely be just after five. As soon as I stick my neck out and tell you to order your favorite dinner at a specific time, instead of me calling you, that would be the day I had to stay late, so, I will call as always."
"Okay. How are things going?"
"Great. We can catch up tonight."
"Bye for now."
"Bye."

***

With the dinner leftovers tucked away in Dacque's refrigerator, Dani and Dacque made themselves comfortable in the living room.
"How is the new job working out?" Dacque asked.

"Really well. The work is a bit different from what I was doing at Max's firm, but similar to the work I did at a couple of other law firms, before I moved to Anywhere. The telephone rings more here than I ever remember it doing in the other offices."

"Do you see much of Max?"

"Oh yes. We have evolved into a full-fledged relationship. I pretty much see him every day, at least for a little while. He does work long hours at times."

"I'm very happy for the two of you. I like Max a lot."

"I'm glad. I certainly do. Changing the subject, I have some interesting news for you."

"I'm listening."

"I know that you do not like to talk about the details from past lives, so I will keep the details to a minimum. In an incarnation where you have not been identified, I had a past life with Max and his mother, but this was not revealed in the information I received through my regression. Max was quite shocked by the information that he received on this particular incarnation. He mentioned the family name to me, and I had the same family name in, apparently, my most recent incarnation. We were generations apart, and neither of us learned the connection in our regression sessions.

"His mother compiles the genealogy in their family and she is the guardian of a box of family trees and photos. It was only after his mother showed me the secrets in her genealogy box, did we realize the connection. His mother handed me an old photo that she had of me from that incarnation, and it must have triggered a past-life recall of some eight years or so where I had resided in the same house with her when she was quite young. It blew my mind.

"I could not believe all of the details that I was able to recall. His mother and I sat there at their dining-room table for well over two hours and recalled numerous events and activities that we shared together. It didn't even seem like it was a previous life to me, it was so clear."

"Hokey Pahokee! That is wonderful. Other than the two group members that I know I mentioned to you, I have never met anyone with past-life recall while in the awake-state."

"It truly was wonderful. It has to be one of my most-treasured experiences. One thing about this still bothers me, though. Max is also a descendant of mine from that same incarnation, and I certainly feel an unexplainable closeness to him, as he does to me, but neither one of us experienced past-life recall. Any ideas why?"

"No idea. It could happen someday down the road. Maybe nothing significant has occurred yet to trigger it. I have read about it in a book or two, but past life recall, while awake, is very rare, and as far as I know, no one has figured out the whys and wherefores. I suspect that when you saw and touched the old photo of you in your previous lifetime, this activated your recall mechanism. Unfortunately, that is about all I can tell you. Certainly keep me posted if you experience any other occurrences. Maybe we can learn something, if it happens a few times."

"I will," Dani assured him.

Chapter 35
Doris' Unforgettable Regression

Doris Winston had been overwhelmed by the Ricker family revelations contained in the regression sessions obtained by Dani and Max. In her mind, it was literally impossible for these revelations to be explained by any possibility, other than past-life recall. It did not take her long to conclude that she needed to check out her own past lives. She telephoned Max on Tuesday evening with the news, but he was busily working away at the office, and gave her Dani's phone number. Dani immediately began to set the process in motion which culminated in Doris and Dani waiting nervously, in Dani's apartment, after lunch on Saturday afternoon, for the imminent arrival of Eyeonthepast.

The suspense was short-lived.

Dani opened the door. "Hello, Eye. You are becoming a regular around here. Come in."

"Hello, Beanpole. Regular is good. It means we are obtaining worthwhile results."

"We definitely are. I'd like you to meet Clippers, our new member."

"Hello, Clippers," Eye said, extending her hand. "Thank you for joining our Reincarnation Enlightenment Group."

Eye wasted no time and, after Dani left the apartment to run some errands, soon had Clippers sinking down into a deep, hypnotic-trance state. "I would like you to picture yourself slowly sliding down a gradually sloping, non-confining tunnel. You see a light at the end of the tunnel, and it gets brighter and brighter as you approach the end. When you exit from the tunnel, you will land in a past lifetime. Let me know when you are out of the tunnel, please?"

"I am out of the tunnel."

"Please describe what you see."

"There is a big celebration or party. Music, food, everyone is having a good time."

"Can you tell me the reason for the celebration?"

"It is our daughter's wedding celebration."

"Please tell me the name of your daughter."

"Blanche. Blanche Woodward. Actually she is now Blanche Ricker."

More Rickers, Eye thought to herself. This family would make an interesting study in reincarnation. Worry about that later.

"Please tell me your name."

"Bernice Woodward."

"If that is your married name, what was your maiden name?"

"Bernice Longsworth."

"What is your husband's name?"

"Nelson, Nelson Woodward."

"What year is it?"

"1885"

"Where is the wedding celebration taking place?"

"In the yard on our farm."

"Please tell me the name of the closest large town, where you go to purchase supplies."

"Macon."

"Is that Georgia?"

"Georgia."

"What is the name of your daughter's new husband?"

"Norman Ricker."

"Before 1885, did Blanche or Norman have any children?"

"No."

"Do you recognize anyone from your current lifetime that was present at the wedding celebration for Blanche and Norman in 1885?"

"Yes."

"Please identify them in 1885, and again today."

"Our daughter Blanche is Dani Christian, and my husband Nelson is Fred Winston."

Eye leaned to her right and removed the CD from the CD player before replacing it with a new one. "I would like you to again picture yourself sliding down the same tunnel as before, sliding towards the light at the end. When you exit from the tunnel, you will land in a different lifetime than the one as Bernice Woodward. Please let me know when you are out of the tunnel."

After a few seconds, Clippers said, "I am out of the tunnel."

"Please describe what you see."

"There is a large crowd, men, women and children, waiting by the side of the path from Capernaum."

"Who are you waiting for?"

"Jeshua."

"Who is Jeshua?"

"Jeshua the healer. Our Savior."

"Are you waiting with the crowd?"

"Yes."

"Is Jeshua a relative or a friend of yours?"
"No."
"Why did you come this day to see Jeshua?"
"I brought our son for Jeshua to heal."
"What is wrong with your son?"
"He has a crippled leg."
"What is your son's name?"
"Abraham, child of Joseph."
"Is your husband Joseph there with you?"
"No."
"What is your name?"
"Anna."

"I would ask you now to move along in time, just a little, to when Jeshua and His followers or disciples arrived at the spot where the crowd, including you and Abraham are waiting. When they arrive there, where you are standing, will you let me know, please?"

"Yes." The room went silent, and the seconds slowly ticked by.

"Four of His followers have joined our waiting group. They are telling us that Jeshua will be arriving in a few minutes. The four followers have split up and are circulating amongst the throng of people. One is coming over where we are. He seems to be looking at us, or maybe it is Abraham that caught his attention.

"'What is the matter with the boy's leg? Did he break it?' he is asking me. I told him that Abraham was born crippled. He has put his arm around Abraham's shoulder and asked us to come along with him. We are moving through the crowd to the edge of the pathway. The people at the south end of the crowd are starting to cheer. I see heads appearing over the knoll. It is wonderful to see Jeshua. We have never seen Him before. He is stopping when He reaches one of His followers. That follower appears to have a blind beggar with him. Jeshua just placed His hand on the beggar's head, and said something quietly. I am too far away to hear. The beggar is jumping up and down, shouting, 'I can see! I can see!' He is now thanking Jeshua.

"They are moving on towards us. The follower beside us is telling Jeshua that Abraham has been crippled from birth. 'Is that correct?' Jeshua is asking Abraham. Abraham says, 'Yes, sir. Please make me well so that I can run and jump like the other boys.' Jeshua is smiling. 'My son, your sins are forgiven. Give Me your crutch.' Abraham hands Jeshua his crutch, and He tosses it on the ground. 'Now My son, let us see you jump as high as you can,' Jeshua says. Abraham is hopping around the path like a rabbit. 'Now,' Jeshua says, 'Let's see you run down to the end of the crowd and back as fast as you can.' Abraham has taken off, moving as fast as I have ever seen any boy run. This is a Miracle. It truly is a Miracle. Abraham has turned around and is charging back towards us. He runs right into Jeshua's arms and is hugging Him, saying, 'Thank you! Thank you!' through his tears.

"The tears are pouring down my cheeks, also. I feel faint. I reach out for Jeshua's follower and he helps me to remain standing. Jeshua backs away from Abraham, and musses-up his hair. 'The Father has Blessed you, My son,' He says and now is walking further down the path. The follower asks if I will be alright, and I tell him I think so. He is also moving along the path, following Jeshua. Abraham and I are hugging each other. We are still crying."

Eye was so mesmerized by the revelation that it took a few moments for it to register that Clippers had stopped talking. 'How do I follow that?' she asked herself. "Is there anyone in your current lifetime that you recognize who is there in the crowd waiting for Jeshua?"

"Yes."

"Please tell me their name then and today."

"Abraham is Max Winston, my son."

"I am now going to slowly bring you out of your hypnotic trance. On the count of ten, you will be wide-awake and feeling refreshed, and you will be able to remember most of what has taken place during our session today. One ...... two ...... three ...... you are beginning to feel more awake, four ...... five ...... six ...... seven ...... you are almost totally awake, eight ...... nine ...... ten. Wake up!"

Clippers stretched her arms, yawned, and opened her eyes.

Eye handed her the two CDs. "I believe that we just experienced the most rewarding regression session that I can ever remember, Clippers. You truly are Blessed."

Chapter 36
Doris' Ecstasy

Doris waited, very impatiently, for Dani to return to her apartment. After Eye departed Doris called Dani's cell phone and told her that her regression session had been memorable, to say the least, but revealed no details. Doris' euphoria was shattered by a charging Dani flinging the apartment door open.

Doris smiled at Dani, but bit her tongue. She knew that it was impossible to conceal the sparkle in her eyes. Dani placed a bag on the dining room table and walked over to the sofa where Doris was seated, and joined her. "Well?"

"In your regression session, did you have an incarnation at the time of Jesus?"

Dani's eyes lit up. "No. Did you?"

"Yes. And it was phenomenal!"

"Damn it!" Dani declared. "And you can't even tell me about it right now, in case I had a past lifetime in those days, and have not yet discovered that incarnation."

"It's a bummer, isn't it?"

"Definitely. Were there any other interesting incarnations that you can tell me about?"

"Yes. More Ricker connections. I was Bernice Longsworth Woodward, the mother of Blanche Woodward Ricker. Know her?"

"Yes!" Dani shouted, and hopped up off of the sofa.

Doris stood up immediately and they leapt into each other's arms. The tears followed, instantly. "It blows my mind how our souls keep showing up over and over in the Ricker genealogy," Doris managed to get out between blubbers.

The soul relatives went through a lot of tissues before the conversation was resumed.

"There's more!" Doris declared. "Your father and my husband, then, was Nelson Woodward, and he just happens to be reincarnated as my Fred."

Dani's jaw dropped. "No way! That is amazing."

"Amazing, but true."

Dani was silent for a short while, trying to process the Ricker family genealogy through her mind. "Correct me where I'm wrong, but it seems that I am the only one of us, or only soul, that shows up just one time in the Ricker-Winston family genealogy. Am I right?"

"Yes, that appears to be true," Doris confirmed. "Fred is Fred and was Nelson Woodward. Max is Max and was Jed Ricker. I am Doris and was Bernice Woodward. You must remember, though, that you, or Blanche, lived a long time, through a lot of generations. Maybe you appeared in earlier generations or ..." Doris paused in mid-sentence, uncertain if she should speak the words her mind was feeding her.

"Or what?" Dani asked.

"Or maybe your part in the Ricker-Winston family genealogy lies in the future? I see the way you and Max look at each other. The sparkle in your eyes! There is an obvious, to an experienced observer, underlying attraction that has brought you two together. I'd bet the kitchen sink that you and

Max will one day add the next generation to the Winston family."

Dani felt herself blush. "Has Max said anything to you that I don't know about? We have only known each other for a few months."

"He has said nothing about this at all, but I know what I see. Someday, down the road, I will remind you of this conversation."

Chapter 37
Cyclone Doris

After her first regression session, Doris was wound up like a spring. She could not wait to check with Max, to see if he had discovered his incarnation at the time of Jesus, but she held herself back, reluctantly, after Dani informed her that Max was working at his office, again. She tore home to poor Fred.

"How did it go?" Fred asked as she flew through the door, feet barely touching the floor.

"Fabulously! And I mean fabulously. Try and imagine the best possible past-life discovery, and it was even better than that."

"Great, tell me about it."

"Fred, don't you remember that I'm not supposed to do that. Dani explained last Sunday why we should not talk about it, especially with anyone who has not had their own regression session. You are going to have one, aren't you Fred? I should say, you are going to have one, Fred!"

Fred laughed. "You have already made up my mind, haven't you?"

Doris laughed with him. "Of course. That shouldn't surprise you after all of these years, my dear."

"Tell me what happened in your session, but exclude the details that I should not know about. Then I'll think about it."

"Stubborn old coot! Okay. I only uncovered two past lives, not three like Dani and Max. I can only speculate why. The second one was so beautiful, and so clear, that it was almost like I was watching a movie. I had an incarnation at the time of Jesus, and I met Jesus."

"No way! You are just trying to talk me into having a session, aren't you?"

"Fred, I'm telling you the truth. I was standing right beside Jesus. If I had stretched out my arm I could have touched Him, but I didn't. There is so much more that I wish I could tell you, and maybe I've already blabbed too much, but that is all I am going to reveal to you about that incarnation. I asked Dani if she had uncovered an incarnation at the time of Jesus, and she said no. I will ask Max the first chance I get, but didn't bother him this afternoon, after Dani told me he was working at the office."

"How did the first past-life pan out?"

"Actually, Fred, it was very informative. Nothing could match the Jesus incarnation, of course, but the first one was pretty great, too. I had another incarnation on the Ricker genealogy tree, and, looking at the big picture, that incarnation now makes perfect sense. That is all that I'm going to tell you. Please, please tell me you will have a session of your own. There is so much interconnection between Max, Dani and I, in our past incarnations that I would be shocked if you did not discover some kind of connection of your own. Stop giving me a rough time. Pick an alias, and we will sign you up for your reincarnation email address. Then I will call Dani and have her register you."

Fred knew perfectly well that he was going to end up having a session whether he really wanted one or not, and, after what Doris had just told him, he had to admit that his curiosity had been piqued. He could string Doris along for a while, just for the heck of it, but decided against that ploy. "Okay, my alias will be Wrench. Let's go find me an email address."

Chapter 38
Lost Connections

Dani walked towards her apartment door, in response to the expected, loud knock. An appointment had been set up, for Fred Winston or Wrench, with Eyeonthepast, for three on Saturday afternoon. Her standing, usual time for visiting the apartment, one o'clock, had already been booked.

"Hello Eye, welcome back, again."

"Hello, Beanpole. Thank you."

"I'm sure you remember Clippers from last Saturday, and this is Wrench, our new member."

Eye shook hands with Wrench. "I am pleased to meet you. Thank you for joining the Reincarnation Enlightenment Group."

"Thank you for having me."

"Are you ready for an unusual adventure?" Eye asked Wrench.

"Yes, I think I am."

Dani and Doris took the clue and headed for the apartment door and their pre-planned shopping adventure. "Call us when you folks are done," Dani teased, "and we will return, if we've run out of money."

"Wonderful," Wrench said, and rolled his eyes.

Eye sprang into action and commenced the process to usher Wrench into a deep hypnotic trance, which, according to plan, should lead him into the recovery of information from some of his past lives. "You are now in a deep hypnotic trance," Eye continued in a gentle, soothing voice. "I would like you at this time to imagine that you are in a non-confining, gently-sloping, downward tunnel, where you can see a light at the bottom. This light will become brighter and brighter as you slide closer to the end of the tunnel. When you reach the end of the tunnel, you will land on your feet in a previous lifetime which has significant connections to your current lifetime. Please let me know when you are out of the tunnel."

A few seconds passed, and Wrench said, "I am out of the tunnel."

"Please describe for me what you see."

"Our daughter and a young man, who lives a few miles from us, have just returned from a horseback ride, and we are sitting at the kitchen table. Our daughter has told us that they want to talk to us about something, and my wife has brought us all a cold glass of water. The young man is saying, 'Mr. and Mrs. Woodward, I am very much in love with Blanche and I have asked her to marry me. She has agreed to be my wife, if you will welcome me into the family. I look at my wife. We smile at each other. We both adore this young man and have been wishing for this day for many months. 'Welcome to the family, son,' I say and offer him my hand. My wife and daughter are hugging each other. All of us are pleased with this development."

"What is your name, Mr. Woodward?"

"Nelson."

"And your wife's name?"

"Bernice."

"Your daughter's name is Blanche, I gather?"

"Yes."

"Please tell me the name of the young man that you have just welcomed into your family."

"Norm Ricker."

Another Ricker, Eye silently thought. Every time I come here there is a Ricker incarnation showing up. I definitely have to look into this further. "Thank you Nelson. I would like you to advance the time, just a little, until the day of the wedding of Blanche and Norm. Please let me know when you are at the wedding celebration, if it indeed does take place."

"We are at the wedding, now."

"What is the year when the wedding takes place?"

"1885."

"Where is the wedding celebration being held?"

"In our yard on the farm."

"What is the name of the closest town to your farm, where you would regularly go for supplies?"

"Macon."

"Is that Georgia?"

"Yes."

"Do you know any people at the wedding celebration that you also know in your current lifetime?"

"Yes."

"Please tell me their names there in Georgia and their names in this lifetime."

"Bernice, my wife, is Doris Winston, my wife in this lifetime. Blanche, our daughter, is Dani Christian."

"Thank you." Eye reached over to her CD player, removed the CD and replaced it with a new one. "I would like you, once again, to imagine yourself back in the tunnel we talked about earlier, sliding down another time towards the light at the bottom. When you exit from the tunnel, you will land in a past lifetime different from your life as Nelson Woodward. Please let me know when you are out of the tunnel."

"I am out of the tunnel."

"Please describe what you see around you."

"We are in a village, a poor village. My wife and I are sad, as our son is preparing to leave us to go off to war, again."

"What is the name of your village?"

"Dunnigan."

"What is the name of your country?"

"The Nation of the Picts."

"What is your name?"

"Enoch Mac Grab."

"What is your wife's name?"

"Bethane Mac Grab."

"What is the name of your son who is going off to war?"

"Jonathan Mac Grab."

"Do you have any other children?"

"Not anymore."

"Please explain what you mean?"

"We had a wee daughter, but the lassie took sick and died. It was many years ago."

"Is Jonathan a soldier for the Nation of the Picts?"

"Yes."

"Do you know who his leader is?"

"King Domnall, King of the Picts."

"Can you tell me what year it is, please?"

"889."

"Can you tell me if Jonathan, or Bethane, or your wee daughter who died, is known to you in this lifetime?"

"Yes. Jonathan, my son, is Max, my son now."

"Thank you, Enoch." Eye once again exchanged CDs in the CD player.

"You are going to take one more journey down the tunnel towards the light, and when you exit from the tunnel you will be in a past lifetime that you have not yet discussed with me today. Please let me know when you are out of the tunnel."

Seconds ticked by in silence. "I am out of the tunnel."

"Please describe for me what you see."

"There is a group of us sitting in a circle. We are eating."

"What are you eating?"

"Fish and berries."

"Where did you get the fish?"

"From the river."

"Did you use a fishing line?"

"What is a fishing line? I do not know fishing line."

"Please tell me the year that it is?"

"What is year? I do not know year."

"Please look at what you and the others are wearing, and describe what you see, for me."

"We are wearing skins from the animals we have hunted."

"How do you hunt the animals?"

"With spear."

"Are you a good hunter?"

"Must be good hunter or soon die."

"Do you know the name of the place where you are now, as you are eating the fish and berries?"

"Beside the river."

"Does the river have a name?"

"Big river down mountain."

"You live in the mountains?"

"In the warm weather."

"Where do you live in the colder weather?"

"In the flat lands."

"In the mountains, where do you sleep at night?"

"In cave."

"In the flat lands, where do you sleep at night?"

"Many different places, near where the animals are."

"Please tell me your name."

"They call me Ugg."

Eye's eyes lit up when she heard the name. Can this really be possible, she wondered? "Ugg, you said there was a group of you together, eating the fish and berries. Is that correct?"

"Yes."

"Are any of the people who are with Ugg, eating fish and berries, known to you in this lifetime?"

"Yes."

"Please identify them."

"You are there."

Eye wanted to dance around the room. I cannot believe that I have discovered someone from that earliest incarnation, she thought to herself. What are the odds? Millions to one? Maybe not! Our past has a strange way of catching up with us. "What was my name when I was there with Ugg?"

"We call you Little One."

This is a blinking miracle! Eye thought she knew the answer to the next question, but it had to be asked. "Were Ugg and Little One just part of the group, or did they have a closer relationship?"

"When night is cold, we sleep close together and ... and sometimes do things, nice things."

Eye was not the least bit shocked. On the contrary, she was thrilled. The information from Wrench's incarnation as Ugg, confirmed the information that she had received many years earlier concerning her incarnation as Little One.

"I am now going to slowly bring you out of your hypnotic trance. On the count of ten, you will wake up, feeling refreshed, and you will remember most of the information that you discovered today from your past lives. One ...... two ...... three ...... four, you are beginning to wake up ...... five ...... six ...... seven, you are now almost completely awake, eight ...... nine ...... ten. Wake up!"

Eye removed the last CD from her CD player, as Wrench stretched and opened his eyes. Eye noticed that he was having difficulty climbing out of Beanpole's recliner, because of his bad back, and took his hands in hers and gave him a tug. They looked into each other's eyes for a long moment and then stepped into each other's open arms. Eye broke into sobs as they held each other tight, and rocked back and forth, slowly, bodies cemented together, once again. Eye eventually released her hold on Wrench, and he followed suit, almost simultaneously. She looked into Wrench's eyes, and could see the tears trickling down his cheeks. "Do you have any idea how many thousands of years our souls have known each other?" she asked.

Wrench nodded, and smiled down at Eye. "I certainly do, Little One, and I am thrilled to discover this incarnation."

They were immediately in each other's arms once again.

Chapter 39
Comparing Incarnations

Fred Winston called Dani's cell phone after Eyeonthepast left Dani's apartment at the conclusion of his remarkable, past-life regression session. Dani and Doris hurried back to the apartment to hear the news. Now that all three of them had experienced their first regression session, they suspected that their respective revelations contained information that could be shared with each other, without prematurely spilling-the-beans.

"I had a Ricker family incarnation, sort of," Fred said. "Doris, you told me you also had one. Were we husband and wife?"

"Yes, and the parents of Blanche," Doris responded. "I already told Dani about it last Saturday, but could not tell you, as you had not experienced your session. My snippet from that incarnation was at Blanche's wedding celebration, in the yard at our farm in Georgia. Yours also?"

"Yes, but it started earlier," Fred advised. "My glimpse involved Blanche and Norm returning to our farmhouse one afternoon, and asking to talk to us. Norm explained that he had proposed to Blanche, and she had said yes, but it was conditional that we approved of the marriage. We both adored Norm and were hoping for that day to arrive, so approval was not an issue. Then Eye advanced me along to the wedding celebration."

"That was interesting," Dani interceded. "I am glad I heard that."

"In my second incarnation, I was in the Nation of the Picts, whatever that was. It was over a thousand years ago. Were either of you there?" Fred asked.

Dani and Doris both shook their heads.

"My final, revealed incarnation was from way, way back in the caveman days. The only person I could identify, that I know in this lifetime, if you can believe it, was Eye."

The ladies found it impossible to conceal their surprise.

"There are details that I could share with you, but maybe I should wait and see what Eye thinks about that. Logically, I have to assume that because I could not identify either of you, or Max, as being incarnated with me at that time, then you must not have been there. It was an interesting incarnation from the standpoint of learning how we lived, way back then, but it could not be described as an earth shattering one."

"It can wait, then," Doris said. "I have already told both of you that my two discovered incarnations were the Ricker one and the Jesus one. I probably should not get into the details of the time-of-Jesus incarnation, as either of you might yet have had an incarnation back then. Dani, didn't you tell me that a friend of yours has discovered over ten past lives?"

"Yes, that is correct," Dani replied. "Both of you, of course, know about my Blanche incarnation, but I should not talk about my other two. When I had my session, I had never met either of you, and would not have been able to identify you even if you were with me in those incarnations."

"That's true," Doris added. "Max has told us about his Jed Ricker incarnation, of course, but he has not mentioned his other discovered incarnations. Did he say anything to you, Dani?"

"One of his other incarnations was with me in England, and he did not mention his third one. Are you two interested in a second regression session? I have been thinking about it, but wanted to wait and see how you two, and Max, made out. Now that we have all had our first session, a second one could possibly be our next move. On the other hand, there is no real rush, I guess. Maybe we should give Eye a few weeks off. We have been working her quite a lot, of late. I'd hate to see her turn us away due to overwork."

"After the incarnation she shared with me," Fred added, "she will always be happy to hear from us. If we have had one incarnation together, is it not suspected that more did or will occur?"

"True, definitely true," Dani confirmed.

Chapter 40
Next Step

Dani called Dacque on Monday evening, to advise him that Max's family had all received their first regression sessions. She minimized the details but did share with him the fact that Doris had discovered an incarnation at the time of Jesus, and that Fred had uncovered an early incarnation with Eye. They also made another, Chinese-food dinner date for Tuesday, at Dacque's apartment.

"After Fred's regression session on Saturday," Dani said, "he, Doris and I spent some time talking about our past lifetimes, within the suggested rules of the Reincarnation Enlightenment Group. There is one really interesting set of incarnations, in the United States, that involve Max's family as well as me. Max and Doris are descendants of their previous incarnations and of Fred in his earlier incarnation. I show up, once, but lived through four generations. That was the incarnation where I experienced the awake-state, past-life recall when Doris handed me my photo from the previous incarnation. Since then, Doris and Fred have discovered their earlier incarnations, and their separate sessions confirmed the details. With Doris also possessing the family genealogy records, we have accumulated a lot of information. We have not, as yet anyway, discovered any connection to you or Eye in those incarnations, but there are some branches on the family tree where knowledge is minimal."

"Just because you, I and Max had an incarnation together in England," Dacque interceded, "does not mean that we will always have incarnations together. And, don't forget that the three of us are, in fact, sharing our current incarnation, and were thrown together, not as relatives, but under some most unusual circumstances."

"Very true," Dani replied. "What do we do next now that Max and his parents have all received regression sessions. Should we be thinking about second sessions, to discover more incarnations as you did, or even a second session elaborating on one of our discovered incarnations, like Doris' incarnation at the time of Jesus? Or, does it make any sense to have a get-together with you and Eye and the four of us? Is it too early for you and Eye to share names or geographic locations with us newcomers, to see if there are possible connections we should investigate? We have lots of questions, lots of possibilities, and could use some answers."

Dacque laughed. "Definitely lots of questions, but questions are good. It is a wonderful indication that all of you are eager to continue your reincarnation enlightenment, as the group just happens to be called. Let me approach Eye concerning your next step. Eye and I also discovered an incarnation together, but no one else in our group appeared to have a connection, at least that I'm aware of. Now, with you, Max and his family, there are six of us souls that have had at least one previous incarnation together. This may even be a new development for Eye. Asking her advice here is probably our next move."

"It is in your hands, my friend."

Chapter 41
Planning The Next Step

As soon as Dani departed for home, Dacque made a beeline for his computer and emailed Eyeonthepast.

Dear Eye
Over the past six weeks or so, you have held four past-life, regression sessions on Saturday afternoons, at the same apartment. The first two were for a young couple, though not actually a couple, around your age, and the most recent two were for an older couple, closer to my age. The older gentleman had a previous incarnation with you.

I just finished a lengthy discussion with one of them, and they as a group are wondering what their next step should be. I said I would discuss it with you. Instead of going back and forth with emails, I would be happier discussing their situation over the telephone, if that is alright with you. I believe you already have my telephone number, from the past, but if you cannot locate it, I will send it again. I look forward to hearing from you, at your convenience.

Sincerely
Streetwalker

Dacque sent-off the email and settled down in front of his television. Within fifteen minutes, his telephone rang.

"Hello."

"Hello, is this Streetwalker?"

"Yes. Hi, Eye. Thank you for calling so promptly."

"My pleasure, Streetwalker. I remember, very well, the four people from the same apartment. I was shocked, but thoroughly delighted, when the gentleman identified one of my incarnations in his reading. The incarnation that you and I shared is the only other time that this has ever occurred."

"I understand, believe me. You may realize that I had an earlier incarnation with some of them, also, and that revelation was a very pleasant surprise to me. The four of them seem quite keen on discovering more information, but are not sure which way to go from here. Should they go for a second session seeking other incarnations, or instead, elaborations on revealed incarnations, like the one with Jesus or with you? They also wondered if a discussion, with you and I included, as we have now both been connected to their souls at least once, would be beneficial? Those were the options that the individual brought up to me. You are the expert in this area. What do you suggest?"

"Truthfully, any of those options would be fine. As you know, I make a CD of every incarnation, but I do not keep any of them. But, I am always alert to the names revealed in each session, so I am pretty sure that I have not been incarnated at the time of any of their currently-revealed, past lives, except the one. It is possible that you were connected more than once, because you had your sessions a few years back. Did you know any of them then?"

"No. That's why the one common incarnation came as a delightful surprise."

"You could hold a group discussion with them, if you wanted to, and it would not be a big shock to me if you discovered other incarnations tied to some of them."

"Certainly that is an option. If we did that, would you like to sit in as a listener or moderator?"

"Actually, I might just like to do that. I'm not sure if you are aware of it or not, but the four of them had one incarnation, or a series of incarnations would be the proper expression, where they were related to each other in their earlier lifetimes. Two or three family names popped up regularly. As you know, I am trying to research just these types of occurrences, and I would be grateful if they would share with me their information on those specific incarnations. If you mention this to them, please make it perfectly clear that their sharing of this information with me is in no way a condition as to whether I grant them future sessions."

"I will definitely make that crystal-clear."

"Thank you. I guess, in summary, any of their suggestions for where they go next, would be acceptable. It is basically a matter of which direction an individual wishes to travel, first."

"I will pass the information on to them, and let them make their choices. Thank you for your call, and for holding all of their sessions in more-or-less rapid succession."

"It is my pleasure. I get almost as big a kick out of their discoveries as they do. It is not work! It's entertainment! Goodnight."

"Goodnight, Eye."

Chapter 42
God's Plan

Dacque called Dani, after his conversation with Eye, and explained that all of the options, which she had outlined for him earlier, were considered by Eye as acceptable. Dacque also informed Dani that Eye had requested permission to conduct some research on the most-common, family connections that were revealed in their sessions, if the family was willing to share it with her. He emphasized that whatever decision they made on this request would have no bearing whatsoever on Eye granting them future sessions.

Dani advised Dacque that she would discuss the options, again, with Max and his parents, and get back to him. The four of them, more or less, agreed that the preferred next-step would be to hold a discovery session which included Dacque and Eye.

Dani cooked-up the brilliant, she thought, idea to have the five of them invited over to Max's mansion for one of his special dinner evenings. Max protested, but was outvoted three to one, and accepted defeat gracefully. The four of them agreed that Saturday evening would be the preferred choice of days, if Eye and Dacque were available, and as it turned out, they were.

Dani chauffeured Dacque and Eye, who congregated at her apartment first, to Max's mansion, but did not reveal the magnitude of the surprise that they had in store. The gate to Max's compound was open, and Dani slowly snaked her way along the driveway and into the clearing.

"Oh my Lord," Dacque declared. "This is where Max lives?"

"This is it! But there is a story behind all of this. Don't be surprised if Max shares it with you."

Dani parked behind another vehicle, which she correctly assumed was Fred's, and the three of them headed up the sidewalk to the front door. Max and his parents had been seated in the right side of the entranceway, where they could see the approaching vehicle, and Max opened the door for his guests before they could ring the bell.

"Come in folks," Max greeted them.

Max closed the door behind them, and Dacque and Eye stood there, frozen, taking-in the spacious, two-story entranceway and horse-shoe-shaped balcony with its art work and numerous closed doors.

"This is really where you live?" Dacque asked. "I never would have pictured you in a place like this."

Max grinned. "I understand. I never would have imagined it, either. To make a long story short, I bought this place because it was an excellent investment opportunity, not because I actually desired to live here."

"I see," Dacque said.

Dani seized the opportunity, provided by a moment's silence, and taking Dacque's arm, ushered him over to Doris and Fred.

"Fred, Doris, I would like you to meet a very special friend of mine. This is Dacque. Dacque, this is Fred and Doris, Max's parents." They shook hands, and Dani continued, addressing Fred and Doris. "It is important, to me, that you understand that Dacque was mainly responsible, apparently with a little help from Above, for Max and I meeting, and ultimately for the enlightening developments that have occurred in the lives of all of us over the past couple of months. Max, have you told them this story?"

"No, I haven't."

"Bear with me, everyone, as I briefly recount how all of this actually got started. One morning, when I was unemployed, depressed and alone here in Anywhere, I took a walk over to MacDunnah Park. I sat down on a park bench to watch the birds, and for whatever reason, I just started to bawl my eyes out. At some point I heard this voice say something like, 'Are you alright, Miss?' I looked up and told this stranger to go away, and he said, 'God told me to help you.' I didn't believe him, of course, but he definitely got my attention. It was Dacque. Nothing about him was the least bit frightening. I assumed at first he was just some senile old fellow with time on his hands. I was wrong. We talked then walked around the park together, and amazingly, I felt much better. He even treated me to lunch. He gave me his card with his name and telephone number on it, and told me I could call him anytime. I didn't even tell him my name.

"The next morning I felt much perkier, and decided to return to the park, actually to the exact same bench, to see if Dacque would show up again, and he did. We walked, talked and lunched again, and my depressed state of mind was noticeably diminished. At some point that morning, I did give Dacque a piece of paper with my cell phone number and Dani, on it. Nothing else.

"The third morning, I did not go back to the park, but instead, resumed my search for a job. As I found out later, that morning Dacque did not return to the park either, but walked instead to the downtown area, and while crossing a street on a green light managed to take a nose-dive into the sidewalk. This nice gentleman in an expensive suit helped him to his feet. Dacque had badly banged-up his right knee and could not walk on it. The nice gentleman, Max, somehow came into possession of the piece of paper with Dani and my phone number on it, and called me with the news of the accident.

"To shorten-up a long story, I drove Dacque to the hospital and after work that evening Max came to the hospital to see how Dacque, a total stranger, was making out with his banged-up knee. That is how Max and I met. At some point later on, after Max had hired me as a temporary fill-in for his secretary, I was telling Dacque how lucky it had been that his accidental tumble had resulted in Max and I meeting, and Dacque stunned me, once again, by saying, 'There are no accidents. That was all part of the plan.'

"I think I went berserk on poor Dacque, but after all that has happened in all of our lives, past and present, over the recent couple of months, I no longer have any doubts about Dacque's declarations. Somehow, for some unknown reason, this has to all be part of God's Plan."

A maid appeared from somewhere behind the staircase. "Mr. Winston, excuse me, but dinner is ready."

Chapter 43
Guardian Angels

After a scrumptious, pork-roast dinner with apple sauce, as requested by Dani, the group of reincarnation enthusiasts migrated to Max's library, so the kitchen staff could clean up for the evening. Dani asked Eye if she would chair their informal get-together and she agreed. Eye asked Dacque, as she had pre-warned him she would, to go through all of his past lifetimes, mentioning only geographic locations and key names, to see if the rest of the assembled group recognized any connections to their revealed incarnations. No new connections were discovered.

Eye then asked if anyone had other questions that they would like to ask. Most of their questions involved what their next step should be.

At the conclusion of the short question-and-answer session, Doris took over. Dani had relayed Dacque's message to Doris that Eye requested access to their Ricker-Winston genealogy and related past-life information, and Doris prepared a copy of her records for Eye. The group moved from their comfortable armchairs to the table in the center of the library, and Doris guided Eye through the current and past-life connections, while the others listened-in attentively.

Doris reached into her genealogy box, and removed an old photograph. "This is a photo of Blanche Woodward Ricker, 1864-1950, Dani's only incarnation in the family, at least that we know of at this time. This was the photo that I handed to Dani, which apparently activated her awake-state, past-life memories of me as a little girl." Doris handed Eye the photo.

Eye looked at it for a few seconds and returned it to Doris.

Doris got up from the table and walked over to where Dani was sitting, beside Max. "Let's see if this works again," she said, and handed the photo to Dani.

Dani clutched the photo to her chest. Everyone waited with baited breath. "I am very old, now. Very feeble. I only get out of bed, now, to go to the bathroom, and often require assistance to make that journey. I am physically and mentally drained. The only real pleasure in my life is the time my little Dorie spends with me. She will often hop up on my bed and spend hours with me, telling me about her day at school or reading stories to me. I often fall asleep before she is finished. How disappointed she must be when that happens." Dani stopped talking and just sat there with her eyes closed.

After an interval of silence, Doris took up the story of Blanche's last days. "I remember those days. My mother had warned me that the Doctor said on his previous visit, that Grandma Blanche might not live much longer. I did not want to hear that, but I was old enough to understand what lay down the road. A couple of weeks later, I think, Grandma Blanche took a turn for the worse, and my mother called the Doctor back in to check her over. When he came out of her room, he said to my mother - I was standing there too - 'She is gone. She went peacefully.' I tore off to my bedroom and cried for hours. Even though I knew it would happen sometime soon, that did nothing to stop the pain that I felt. It was in the evening, after dinner, and my mother came in to my room a time or two to check up on me, but what could she do? I cried myself to sleep.

"Sometime during the night, something woke me up," Doris continued with her recollections. "I looked over at the side of my bed, and Grandma Blanche was sitting there smiling at me. She looked much younger, much younger than I had ever remembered her, but I recognized her right away. She said, 'Don't cry, my little sweetheart. I'm fine now.' She stood up and did a perfect pirouette beside my bed, and I suddenly realized that I could see right through her. She returned to the side of my bed, and said, 'There is someone here with me I think you will be happy to see.' This man in a bright, white uniform walked over from the end of my bed and stood beside Grandma Blanche. I recognized him, immediately. 'Daddy? Is that really you, Daddy?' I asked. He smiled that full-toothed grin that I always remembered, but he did not say anything. I realized that I could see right through him, as well. I didn't really understand what was happening, but I was not afraid, either. Grandma Blanche said, 'Close your eyes and go back to sleep, my sweetheart. We will be here to watch over you.' Then poof, they both disappeared.

"I closed my eyes," Doris continued, her voice quivering as she fought back tears, "and I eventually fell off to sleep again. I knew that I was going to miss my Grandma Blanche, terribly, but it felt so much better knowing that I had two Guardian Angels who loved me, and were going to take special care of me."

Chapter 44
Could You Have Imagined?

At the conclusion of the memorable evening at Max's estate, Dani chauffeured Eye and Dacque back to her apartment building, where their vehicles were parked. Eye thanked Dani for the ride, and hurried on her way. Dacque tarried awhile, and he and Dani chatted outside, in the delightfully-cool, evening air.

Dacque turned towards his car, then stopped and circled to face Dani. "Could you have ever imagined, when we first met in MacDunnah Park, and you told that interfering old man, politely, mind you, to get lost, that your life could possibly progress to this point in six months?"

"Never in a million years," Dani replied, and gave Dacque a quick hug. "I make it a habit not to dwell on it, but sometimes I do wonder how different my life would be today, if God had not steered you to 'our bench,' that day in the Park. I am so blessed to have you in my life."

"You have certainly brought much sunshine into my life," Dacque added. "God's wonders never cease. It will be exciting to discover what He has planned for us for our next six months, or six years."

"One thing we can count on - it won't be dull."

"You've got that right."

Watch for the publication of
Soul Rescue -
Book II of the Dacque Chronicles

Meet the Author

Doug Simpson is a retired high school teacher who has turned his talents to writing. His first novel, a spiritual mystery titled Soul Awakening, was published in the United States in October of 2011, by Book Locker. His magazine and website articles have been published in 2010 to 2012 in Australia, Canada, France, India, South Africa, the United Kingdom, and the United States. His articles can be accessed through his website at http://dousimp.mnsi.net.

Author Contact Info:
Website - http://dousimp.mnsi.net.
Twitter - https://twitter.com/#!/1DougSimpson
https://www.facebook.com/doug.simpson.902
jesuscayce@yahoo.com

Made in the USA
Charleston, SC
21 March 2013